KRIS LONGKNIFE'S MAID GOES ON STRIKE & OTHER SHORT STORIES

VIGNETTES FROM KRIS LONGKNIFE'S WORLD

MIKE SHEPHERD

KL & MM BOOKS

COPYRIGHT INFORMATION

Kris Longknife's Maid Goes on Strike
& Other Short Stories
Vignettes from Kris Longknife's World
by
Mike Shepherd

Published by KL & MM Books
eBook Published October 2017
Print Book Published December 2017
Copyright © 2017 by Mike Moscoe

All rights reserved. No part of this book may be reproduced or transmitted in any form or by any electronic or mechanical means, including photocopying, recording or any other information storage and retrieval system, without the written permission of the publisher.

This book is a work of fiction set 400 years in humanity's future. Any similarity between present people, places or events would be spectacularly unlikely and is purely coincidental.

This book is written and published by the author. Please don't pirate it. I'm self-employed. The money I earn from the sales of these books allows me to produce more stories to entertain you. I'd hate to have to get a day job again. If this book comes into your hands free, please consider going to your favorite e-book provider and investing in a copy so I can continue to earn a living at this wonderful art.

I would like to thank my wonderful cover artist, Scott Grimando, who did all my Ace covers and will continue doing my own book covers. I also am grateful for the editing skill of Lisa Müller, David Vernon Houston, Edee Lemonier, and, as ever, Ellen Moscoe.

Ver 1.0

Bowker eBook ISBN-13: 978-1642110180
Bowker Print Book ISBN-13: 978-1642110227
Amazon Print Book ISBN-13: 978-1974579013

ALSO BY MIKE SHEPHERD

Published by KL & MM Books

Kris Longknife: Emissary

Kris Longknife: Admiral

Kris Longknife's Relief

Kris Longknife's Replacement

Rita Longknife in the Jump Point Universe

Rita Longknife: Enemy Unknown

Rita Longknife: Enemy in Sight

Ace Books by Mike Shepherd

Kris Longknife: Mutineer

Kris Longknife: Deserter

Kris Longknife: Defiant

Kris Longknife: Resolute

Kris Longknife: Audacious

Kris Longknife: Intrepid

Kris Longknife: Undaunted

Kris Longknife: Redoubtable

Kris Longknife: Daring

Kris Longknife: Furious

Kris Longknife: Defender

Kris Longknife: Tenacious

Kris Longknife: Unrelenting

Kris Longknife: Bold

To Do or Die: Jump Point Universe Book 4

Vicky Peterwald: Target

Vicky Peterwald: Survivor

Vicky Peterwald: Rebel

Mike Shepherd writing as Mike Moscoe in the Jump Point Universe

First Casualty

The Price of Peace

They Also Serve

Short Specials

Kris Longknife: Training Daze

Kris Longknife : Welcome Home, Go Away

Kris Longknife's Bloodhound

Kris Longknife's Assassin

The Lost Millennium Trilogy Published by KL & MM Books

Lost Dawns: Prequel

First Dawn

Second Fire

Lost Days

KRIS LONGKNIFE'S MAID GOES ON STRIKE

You knew this had to happen. Sooner or later, Abby was going to have to strike out on her own. With Granny Rita going crazy, it all seemed like a good idea at the time.

This story is a bridge between Kris Longknife's Replacement and Kris Longknife's Relief.

KRIS LONGKNIFE'S MAID GOES ON STRIKE: LIFE ON ALWA STATION

Abby Nightingale leaned back in her desk chair and sighed. She was finally done.

Her desk was clean – as much as it ever was. Her in-baskets, both real and virtual, were either empty or tapped down enough that they wouldn't catch fire for at least two weeks. She could finally walk away from her job and enjoy two weeks' vacation. She had the papers signed, sealed, and printed out in her purse.

"I'm a free woman," she shouted joyfully, but very softly.

Abby's office was right next door to Pipra Strongarm's executive suite. Being this close to the CEO of most of the industrial production in the Alwa system, all the way on the hell and gone on the other side of the galaxy from human space, often facilitated free and open communications.

Just now, that was the last thing Abby wanted.

If she hurried, she could just catch the final shuttle of the day down to Memphis on the Columbia River in Rooster territory. In three hours, she could be at her shared plantation, in General Steve's arms, and loving it.

Make it two hours, if he met her at the shuttle landing dock at Memphis.

Considering Steve's lusty nature and the six weeks since their last vacation, she was betting on him meeting her at Memphis.

Abby grabbed her small, overnight bag from beside her door, turned out the lights and was halfway across the empty outer office in a flash. Everyone else had gone home long ago.

She'd almost made it to the door when she got caught.

"Abby, get your butt back here and in my office," came in a voice that was better at sultry and sexy, but at the moment was shouting a command.

"Boss lady, I got two weeks' vacation that I damn near had you sign in blood. I'm out of here," Abby answered back, but she was standing in place, no longer running for the shuttle.

"Abby Nightingale, get your damn ass back here, now!" showed some serious intent. Pipra was usually very soft spoken when she gave Kris Longknife's former maid directions. This was starting to sound like a Level Red 3 crisis. The only thing higher than a Red 3 crisis was a Granny Rita crisis.

Abby dropped her bag and turned to meet her fate. Quickly, she was at the door to Pipra's office. "Boss, you do recall that in my last job, I killed a whole lot of people while keeping Kris Longknife alive."

"And here I thought you washed her hair," was Pipra's oft repeated comeback to Abby's oft repeated threat.

"Wash her hair. Shoot an assassin. Make the body disappear. All in a good five minutes' work around her royal pain in the ass."

Pipra motioned Abby to the visitor's chair beside her

desk and the former maid slipped into the seat she warmed way too much these days.

"It's your hands-on experience with Longknifes that I need," Pipra said, handing a message flimsy across to Abby, "Granny Rita is at it again,".

Abby groaned, even before she set eyes on the message. "Granny Rita!"

"Yeah. Rita Nuu Longknife to some of us."

"What's she gone and done now?" Abby said, scanning an unusual message. It was all in fancy calligraphy!

Pipra said nothing, so Abby did her best to adjust her eyes to an ancient format of letters with flowing language to match.

One word drew her eyes. A word that hardly belonged imbedded among such archaic language and fonts. "Nationalize!"

Abby's eyes shot up to stare in horror at her boss.

Pipra was grinning back at her. "Is *that* a good enough reason for you to miss your shuttle?

"But she can't do that!" Abby insisted. "Even Kris Longknife never tried to do anything like that. Nobody is that stupid!"

Pipra handed Abby another flimsy. This seemed to be the same message in a readable font. "That says she thinks she can. Note what I highlighted."

In yellow was a section where Granny Rita proclaimed:

BY THE POWERS VESTED IN ME AS VICEROY OF KING RAYMOND OF THE UNITED SOCIETY TO THE VARIOUS PEOPLES OF THE PLANET ALWA, I DO PRONOUNCE AND PROCLAIM THE CONFISCATION AND NATIONALIZATION OF ALL MEANS OF PRODUCTION USED BY HUMANS IN THE ALWA

SYSTEM EXEMPTING ONLY THOSE ON THE PLANET ITSELF.

Pipra leaned forward in her chair. "I've got my computer researching the history of nationalizations, but she hasn't come up with much. You think yours can do better?"

"Mata Hari?" Abby asked. Abby, as a result of her close and uncomfortable work with Kris Longknife, had been one of the first recipients of one of the Magnificent Nelly's kids. Mata Hari, a name left over from when Abby was as much a spy as an assassin or a hair washer, was sentient. Unlike her mother, she had never shown a desire to argue with Abby or tell horrible jokes. Her occasional humor was usually quite tasteful as well as funny.

"Nationalization was a practice among smaller nations," Abby's computer began to immediately report, "that developed during the latter half of the twentieth century as colonial powers retreated, although a major power might, indeed, have a radical change in government that brought on nationalization, but usually only for a short time. It has been rarely used since the diaspora into space. Its last significant usage was on the planet Savannah. They nationalized all off-planet ownership in order to delegitimatize some of the more egregious actions of the Unity Government before its collapse after the Unity War. This sort of nationalization was then declared unconstitutional on Savannah in order to gain off-planet investment. Rita Nuu Longknife was heavily involved in that investment and may have been the source of the constitutional amendment."

"Damn," Pipra breathed. "The old biddy's dug deep into her bag of tricks to come up with this stinking pile of shit."

Abby raised both eyebrows. Her boss was definitely stressed out by this one. Why wouldn't she be? When Kris

Longknife was called back to human space, Pipra had been dumped with running an industrial empire that stretched from the mining operations in the asteroid belt all the way to the production fabrication plants on Alwa's one large moon. Oh, hell, had Rita also nationalized the space stations and the starship building yards on them as well?

The king had sent out the first yards and made sure they were civilian activities even if all of the managers were retired senior Navy officers. At the time of their arrival, Kris Longknife had been, at best, a commander. She would have quickly been outranked by a Navy force.

Had that previously good idea just born poisoned fruit?

"Abby, get down to Refuge. You've spent more time with Longknifes and the corkscrews that pass for their brains than anyone on staff. See what you can make of this and get this withdrawn. We sweat blood to come up with the latest rebalancing of production to get the most for defense, consumer goods, and industrial investment. I don't want to have to go through all that again because one old lady pulled the rug out from under our feet."

Pipra leaned back in her chair and scowled at the ceiling. "Our production effort is held together with spit, glue, and bailing wire. We've got over half a dozen different corporations now making up our consortium. If they don't think I'm doing a good enough job for them, they'll have my head for a hood ornament even if I do have the largest interest and I represent Nuu Enterprises. Understand?"

"This she-bull in the China shop can wreck everything," Abby concluded.

"You got it, gal. Now, go get 'em tiger."

"Go get a Longknife?" Abby snorted. "Nobody, even the Peterwalds, have ever succeeded in mounting a Longknife head over their mantelpiece."

"No head required," Pipra said. "Just walk her back from this. Find out what she wants. Figure out a way to get it for her without all this mess. Whatever."

Abby stood. "On my way, Boss. But you owe me. You own me an extra week's vacation."

"What's the big rush?" Pipra said. "You and that soldier boy of yours aren't going to start a baby or anything like that, are you?"

Abby dodged the question. "That *man* is a *Marine*."

"Yeah, yeah. Whatever. Run. I've got them holding the last shuttle to Refuge for you."

Abby ran. Yes, a dumb manager could hold a shuttle, but if it missed its drop window, it would just have to ride the station around for another orbit and be ninety minutes later.

Abby hailed a cab at the shuttle port. A few years back, the shuttle landing had been a floating dock serviced by a few electric jitney cabs.

Now, the shuttle dock had a pair of hangers serviced by a solid concrete ramp up from the lake as well as a major T-pier that could handle two or three longboats at a time tied up alongside. The cabs were now fully electric cars good for sixty miles an hour on roads that weren't so rutted that they'd shake the passengers' eyeteeth out.

A lot had changed in the four years since Granny Rita had brought Abby down, at Kris Longknife's elbow, to see *her* town.

Abby saw all around her that the city of Refuge had changed as well. The surviving human colonials had been scratching out a bare subsistence on the land given to them by the local, bird-like Alwans. Now they had two harvests in the granaries and were living as comfortably as any human in a startup colony. Adobe mud buildings were being replaced by perma-plastic and steel buildings. A six-story building was going up at Alwa University.

Yes, the times were a-changin'.

The woman known as Rita Nuu Longknife, Commodore Longknife, or Granny Rita, may have aged over the years; however, she certainly didn't seem to have changed. This so-called Proclamation of Confiscation and Nationalization alone said the old gal hadn't lost a bit of her bite.

The drive to Government House was much longer than Kris Longknife's ride, even though Abby took it at a much faster pace. The old Government House was now relegated to a City Hall for Refuge. Ada's new Government House was on the outskirts of town. Though, if the city kept growing, it would likely be the center of town soon enough.

The cab pulled up to the back of Government House. There was a Rooster waiting at the curb. He paid the cab driver in Colonial script and then motioned the human to follow him into the working entrance to the Colonial capital building. He led her up a flight of stairs, then down a dimly lit hallway before stopping to open a door for Abby.

Abby stepped into a cluttered office that would have fit any number of worried people in human space. Except for the specifics of the large map on the wall, it could have been fit for a government official, business manager, or truck dispatcher.

Ada didn't look up from the reader she was looking at. "This better be good. I was actually going to have dinner with my husband and kids today. My mom was even coming over. They reserved today a week ago. Said something about it being my birthday."

Now the First Minister of the Colonial Government looked up at Abby and scowled. "You didn't say why you were in such an all fired hurry to see me or give me a reason I should. There aren't many people who would get me to jump just on their say so. Please tell me that I'll soon be scratching your name off the list of people who would never waste my time."

Abby settled into the chair next to Ada's desk, the one she had not been offered. "Have you seen Granny Rita's latest?"

"Good God, not her. I thought she'd been too quiet lately. What's the old gal gone and done this time?"

Abby handed over the lovely calligraphed declaration.

Ada's scowl got even deeper as she eyed the document. "I've never seen such scribble in my life. What's it say?"

Abby handed across the proclamation in plain font.

Ada scanned it quickly, eyed Abby, then read it a bit more slowly. Then she looked up and frowned at the woman from the other side of the galaxy. "Please tell me this doesn't mean what it seems to be saying. Oh, God, please."

"Are you asking if that rambling collection of fancy words means that Granny Rita has just taken control of all the means of production in the Alwa system except for those located on the lovely mud ball under your feet? The answer, according to my computer and my ancient degree in Business Administration, is yes." Before Abby could go on, Ada interrupted her.

"She can't do that." was a lot more definite than the, "Can she?" that followed.

Abby shrugged. "She says she can. She says as King Ray Longknife's viceroy on Alwa she can do just that."

Ada launched into a long stream of expletives that would make even a Marine's ears burn. Abby knew. She'd been on a drop mission or two that hadn't gone according to plan. They ended with, "Get me a drink. Some of that single malt whiskey. The three-year-old bottle."

Abby found a bottle and two dirty glasses. She wiped them out with a stray paper napkin and poured them half full.

Ada shook her head as she took the glass. "I knew when Granny Rita asked us to vote her co-viceroy, just for Alwa, she said, that we were making a mistake. That damn dame hated Ray Longknife. Why would she ever want to be his viceroy?"

Eighty years ago, at the end of the Iteeche War, Rita Nuu Longknife had been married to Ray Longknife. She'd also commanded a battlecruiser squadron that beat back an Iteeche invasion fleet. She'd killed a lot of good Iteeche Marines and really pissed off the Iteeche Navy. They had chased her until her velocity was so high that when she and her two remaining ships hit an unmarked jump, she'd been shot well across the galaxy. A few more highly improbable jumps, and she was hacking the ice armor off of one battlecruiser to give the other ship enough reaction mass to slow down.

Alwa was the system they finally came to rest in.

Rita had been a harsh taskmistress as she drove her crew to do what they needed to survive. She hadn't been averse to using a hangman when she had to. She was remembered by the survivors from those days not fondly, but respectfully.

As a kind of wedding present, Kris Longknife had managed to get a vote out of the local Colonial assembly to make her Viceroy. Only Rita could have gotten the same vote without tying a knot with someone again.

The argument she presented was simple. She'd share the duties with the newly assigned Grand Admiral Sandy

Santiago, new commander of the Navy on Alwa Station. Sandy would be the viceroy from King Ray for everything above the atmosphere, and Rita would be the viceroy from King Ray for everything dirtside. It would all work out just fine.

The problem was that Grand Admiral Santiago had taken off to try to regularize relations with the other aliens they'd stumbled upon, the cats who had their claws on the button for nuclear weapons. At the time, it seemed like a good idea

Now? Not so much.

Ada tapped her commlink. "Kuno, get in here. If you can find Lago, get him, too."

"On my way, chief," came back immediately.

Ada took a long swig off her drink, then leaned back in her chair and stared at the ceiling. "Can a government actually walk off with the whole kit and caboodle, lock, stock and barrel?"

"They ain't done it recently, but yeah, it's been done in the past. Hell, didn't Kris do something like that? Didn't she have you claim that you'd given the Alwans the right to all the natural resources in the system so Ray and the lawyer types that came out with him for that one visit couldn't latch onto them for themselves?"

"I seem to have the original of that proclamation around here somewhere," Ada admitted. "Still, that was to keep us and the birds from being robbed blind by you interlopers. This?"

"Is Granny Rita robbing the interlopers of everything, including their underwear?" Abby answered.

Ada's Pretorian guard began to arrive. Lago was a young Rooster; he still had his first mating plumage along what passed for arms and legs. The other two were humans, one tall and dark, the other short and fair. Abby knew them for Kuno, who coordinated Mining, and Baozhai, who was the colonial's treasurer, which was one tough job since taxes were still paid in kind.

The government's paper "work" script was still not all that respected.

Ada quickly filled them in on Granny Rita's latest hijinks. All three of them just shook their head. Ada finished with a question. "Can that old biddy do this? I don't remember any place in her warrant as downside Viceroy where we gave her that kind of power. Do any of you?"

All three shook their heads, but Kuno was going through his reader even as he shook his head.

"I've got the official commission the Senate voted on," he said. "Let's see. I thought we tied it down pretty specifically. Everyone knows that woman would drive an elephant through a mouse hole."

That got nods of agreement from all of the Colonials. Abby just raised an eyebrow. She'd been around when Kris Longknife drove space ships through tiny cracks in the pavement. She'd learned the hard way to never trust a Longknife.

"Where's this warrant you gave her as downside Viceroy?" the former Longknife employee asked.

Lago had it up on the wall as the screen that had been showing a map of human land use on Alwa vanished. In its place was a long proclamation with only a few letters, those starting paragraphs, in calligraphy. The rest was easily readable.

Abby began to read through it slowly.

"Uh oh," Kuno said. "Check out the ending of Paragraph 8. Was that sentence in any of the drafts we discussed?"

Ada read it slowly. "The Viceroy shall likewise be

charged with securing the safety of all Colonials in their abodes, no matter where they reside." The first minister looked at her own reader.

She scowled and scanned through several pages of her reader. "I've got six different draft versions of paragraph 8. None of them had anything after 'Securing the safety of all Colonials.' Where'd that 'in their abodes, no matter where they reside' come from?"

All three of her staff had been there when the warrant had been negotiated. Each one studied their own notes. Baozhai pulled out another reader and began paging through it hurriedly.

At the end of a long five minutes, all four of the Colonials found themselves staring blankly at each other.

"Hold it," Baozhai said. "This thing she added on is in conflict with the other commissions we gave to her and Admiral Santiago. Rita got authority dirtside. Sandy has authority in space."

"Yeah," Kuno said, "but it's in her warrant anyway. Where native Alwans abide, she has authority and we've got a lot of Roosters and Ostriches abiding on both the space stations and moon. I think most ships have Alwans and there are even some Ostriches out in the asteroid belt."

The four went back to staring at each other.

Ada finally turned to Abby and summed it up for all of them. "That old fart pulled one over on all of us. Do you think she was planning this nationalization scam from the first day production fabs began to show up here?"

"I'll have to ask her," Abby said.

"When?" Ada asked.

"As soon as she'll see me. Mata, connect me to Granny Rita."

"Hi, Abby. I figured you'd be the sacrificial lamb they'd

send over to talk to me. You do remember, I've still got the old hangman's phone number on speed dial, don't you?"

"I'd expect nothing less from a Longknife," Abby answered.

"Oh, now you're just being mean. I ain't been a Longknife for nigh on ninety years. I finally washed all the blood off from my misspent youth quite a few years ago."

"Whatever. We need to talk."

"Drop by any time."

"I'm on my way," Abby said.

"I'll keep the light on for you," and the line clicked off.

"Do I need to call out the guard to form an armed escort for you?" Ada asked. Abby suspected the bureaucrat was at least partially serious.

"Nope, but if I'm not back in three hours, I'd be mighty grateful if you'd mount a rescue mission."

"You got a deal."

A cab was waiting for Abby as she left Government House. When she asked if he knew were Granny Rita lived, he just laughed.

"Everyone knows where Commodore House is."

The drive took Abby along a road around the edge of Refuge. If she didn't know better, she'd think that the New Government House had been intentionally built to be as far from Commodore House as they could get it. Much of the drive had city buildings to her left and open fields to her right. Finally, they turned down a gravel road and approached a wood. Driving through it, Abby realized that the forest had been planted over the years to form rings. Nearer the main road were small saplings, new planted to ten or twenty years old. Then the trees jumped to taller, forty-year-old trees. Finally, they drove through tall Earth cedars and spreading oaks seventy to eighty years old that must have been planted just after the survivors made planet fall.

The birds had given the humans only the worst land they had: dry, barren, hard scrabble ground. The colonials had struggled to make any of it decent. For this strange, layered stand of trees to be this rich and this tall meant someone had devoted a lot of effort as time and land became available.

They came out of the woods to see a large building standing on a slight rise. Commodore House was in the form of an H made of adobe bricks topped with red roof tiles. The horizontal bar which looked the most weathered, was two stories. The four wings coming out from its edges were three or four stories high. The different colored adobe of each wing, as well as different roof tiles showed that they been added at different times and with a slightly different designer involved.

There were other one and two-story additions growing out of the two tall vertical wings. These also looked like the most recent add-ons.

The cab took Abby to a two-story addition that formed a horizontal addition to the bottom of the north wing and slowed to a halt.

"I'll wait for you. You won't get a cab out this far this late at night."

Abby dug into her purse for a tip, but the cabby waved her off. "They paid me before you got in. Don't worry about it."

Abby thanked him and headed for the broad, white-painted door. There was only a door handle, no lock, and no knocker. Abby rapped on the door and waited. She was about to rap again when she heard the sound of a wooden bolt being lifted. A moment later, the door opened and Granny Rita, herself, peeked around the door.

"Hi, Abby. What brings you here this late in the evening?"

"A little of this, a bit of that," the former maid and assassin said, vaguely.

"Oh, that, huh? Hi, Howard," she said, waving at the cabby. He waved back.

"He going to wait for you?"

"That's what he told me."

"I can put you up for the night."

"Nope. I had two weeks leave approved and I'm burning one day of that right now. I hope we can get this problem resolved and I can get over to see my husband."

"General Bruce and you have a place outside of Memphis, don't you?" Granny Rita said, inviting Abby in.

There was a foyer with a mat to wipe muddy feet on. Off to the right was an open door leading to a cluttered office. Off to the left was open space forming a kind of sitting room, big enough for a medium size meeting. Rita pointed Kris Longknife's former maid in that direction and she settled into a wooden rocker across from another one. The walls and floors were lovely sawn wood, a bit rough on the finish, but the women Abby had worked for on old Earth would have paid a medium size fortune for something half as good.

A young girl, maybe fifteen, likely six months pregnant, brought a tea serving for two out and put it on the table between the two of them.

"Can I get you anything else, Granny Rita?"

"Maybe some of those shortbread cookies your granny

makes," Rita said and the gal scampered off. *Pregnancy has got to be for the young.*

"She's one of my great-great-great granddaughters," Rita said by way of explanation. "Once Commodore House was full of three or four generations, but now, most of the older folks have moved out to their own places. I get the occasional boy or girl that can't stand to stay home one more minute. Sometimes they come with friends. Sometimes they come with a kid on the way like Alana there. The house is more a hotel than a home anymore, but I love them no matter why they come. So, you the sacrificial virgin they sent out to feed this rampaging old dragon?"

"I ain't been a virgin for a long time, you old biddy, and you ain't no dragon. Though I think you are an old fool."

"Old fool?"

"We had everything calmed down and running smoothly, then you had to run a truck full of manure right into the family's Sunday dinner."

Rita took time to pour the tea, then hand Abby a cup and took one for herself. She blew on it, touched it to her lip, and frowned. "Too hot. I take it you're talking about my nationalization decree?"

"The selfsame."

"What's not to like about it?"

"You know it's a bitch for us to balance out competing demands, then level resources so we get the closest we can to full production and happy customers. Before Kris left, we worked out a nice balance that gave consumer goods a bit of a lead over defense and left just enough over to grow production to keep ahead of both our growing human population and the number of birds that want into our economy. You were there! You know we sweated blood and Kris

Longknife chewed a lot of our asses before we settled on the production schedule."

"I do remember," Rita said, and tried her tea again. Abby's was untouched and still cooling.

"Then why did you jump into the middle of this and what do you think you're gonna get out of it? For God's sake, woman, this is just plain dumb."

"What if I told you I don't intend to jigger anything?"

"Then why do this? You got people all riled up and no one knows your agenda. It's just plain damn fool stupid."

Rita took a tiny sip, found it to her liking and took a deeper swallow. She nodded toward Abby's cup and the visitor tried a taste.

"Chamomile tea. You knew this was gonna be a bitch of a meeting."

"I figured as much," Rita admitted.

"You want to tell me what you think you've done and why it's worth all the howling I'm hearing from here to the asteroid belt?"

"Were you there when that new management team my spoiled brat of a son sent out here to run things arrived?"

"I was with Pipra when they busted in and told her to pack up her desk and get lost, yeah."

"Assholes. But who can you expect an asshole to hire? Yeah. Were you there when they met our honorable former Viceroy, Her Highness Admiral Kris Longknife?"

"I helped Pipra persuade them that they should pay their respects to the only shareholder of Nuu Enterprise's preferred voting stock before they got too far into their plans to change everything. They were wanting to strip farms to extinction for that magic plant down south that's worth trillions because it will remake nano tech. My boss deputized me to be their seeing eye dog and get them over to Kris."

"How'd it go?"

Abby snorted. "Not at all like *they* intended. I know Pipra had called ahead. Kris was way pregnant. Her feet hurt and her legs were swollen. She was not at all ready to suffer fools. But you got to give her credit. She let them hang themselves. She got them talking and then sat back and listened to them."

Abby shook her head. Kris Longknife did know how to set traps – for alien monsters or stupid thieves. "It took about two shakes of a lamb's tail before they were strutting around telling her how they were going to make a fortune for your bratty son and all Nuu Enterprise shareholders. She gave them rope. They took the rope, tied it in a fine noose, and hung it so prettily around their necks. Then she strung them up high. They hardly knew what hit them and were still hollering as Marines hustled them off to the brig."

"I would have loved to have been there and seen that," Rita said.

"I could have made a fortune selling tickets, but having a bleacher full of paying customers might have given away Kris's hand."

"No doubt. So, what do we do when the next ship of fools arrives from my son and tries to ruin it for everyone else?"

"It may be a while," Abby said. "Kris pretty much stripped them down to brig jumpsuits and put them on a returning merchant ship that won't make planetfall until it gets to Chance. Those folks at Chance really do believe in no such thing as a free lunch. It will be interesting to see if any of those big boss types can find a job there that pays more than digging ditches. Certainly no one's going to spot them the money for an interplanetary message. I figure those dudes will be a long time earning enough to phone home for help. Meanwhile, your boy Alex will be fat, dumb, and happy, figuring he's running things here and he ain't."

Abby and Rita shared a laugh, whether it was at six suits struggling to find a real job or having to do an honest day's work or Alex being cut out of the loop, they didn't bother to clarify.

"But," Granny Rita said when their mirth ran down, "I still ask, what do we do when the next bunch of fools show up? Next time it might not be Alex. It could be any one of the half dozen plus conglomerates that we've got working as a team here that compete against themselves back in human space.

Rita paused to reflect for a moment. "We're functioning as a collective. We have to do it that way out here on the tip of the spear. How much you want to bet that the folks who spent the money for our initial fabrication plants are going to want a return on investment sooner rather than later?"

Abby had to admit, it was a good question. "Still, what can folks back on the other side of the galaxy expect to get from us out here? The shipping costs for pretty much anything will price just about anything we ship back there right out of their market. Wood like your lovely house is made of might bring a small fortune if it could be sold back on Earth, but there are plenty of forests a lot closer to home that can meet Earth's needs."

Abby shook her head. "The only reason we're here is to be a stalking horse for the damn aliens. King Raymond got the stuff sent out here to make us look like a real going concern, a serious industrial economy, so when the aliens take us down, they'd figure they got all of us. Kris being Kris turned what was supposed to be a Potemkin village into one tough nut that they can't crack and now we do what we have to do to live out here. They've got to consider us a charity case, not a profit center."

"Honey, I know these types. I met them when I was still sitting on my daddy's knee. Everything is a profit center with them. No. They're going to do their damndest to pluck this turkey. We got to make our turkey so damn mean and ornery that they don't dare risk going for a feather for fear of losing a finger."

Abby thought for a moment, and couldn't see a flaw in Granny Rita's basic argument.

"I worked for some real tightwads back on old Earth. I guess I've wiped the decrepit asses of some of the self-same folks your daddy introduced you to. Still, Rita, this was not well done. You've tossed your old body right into the middle of the punch bowl and there are too many people who remember when you solved your problems by stringing people up. You've burned too many bridges for anyone here to be happy with you standing in the middle of our damn bridge."

Rita leaned back and rocked for a few moments. "So, you like my solution. You just don't like me doing it."

"Basically, yeah."

Rita shook her head slowly. "Name me someone who could pull this off. Ada? She's too nice. Your Pipra? They bulldozed her already. Your Grand Admiral Santiago? She's Navy and her being boss girl of our industry smacks of a military junta. No, I'm sorry Abby, but it's either this ornery old cuss or it don't get done."

Abby sipped her tea as the two women rocked quietly for a few minutes. What with Rita's longevity treatments, the two of them didn't look all that different in age. Abby had had a hard life growing up in the slums of New Eden, then did what she had to do to earn her way off planet.

She'd done what she had to for a very long time and it cost her.

The same could be said of the woman rocking across from her. Rejuvenation had tightened and softened her skin. She could pass for forty rather than her hundred plus years. Still, Rita had done what she had to do to hold together a struggling colony.

The problem here, was that Rita's sins followed her around like the chains on Marley's ghost on some Christmas Eve night. People remembered.

The survivors had put up with it because, in their own hearts, they'd known they had to accept Rita's hard rule or go down under an onslaught of misfortunes that any generous god would never have allowed one small group of humanity to suffer.

They'd put up with her then, but no one wanted to put up with her now.

In the natural order of things, old people died and their sins were interred with their bones. Now, old bones got to dance around at weddings and births, naked in their sin, and folks were trying to figure this new way out.

Rita needed to retire from public life.

Fat chance of that happening, Abby thought as she finished her tea.

The visitor stood. "I'd best be going. I need to talk to some folks, pass along your intent to 'em, and see if I can calm them down. Rita, it would have gone down better if you'd included a few folks in your thinking before you shoved us all off this cliff."

"And if I had, they'd have voted me out of my Viceroy job and this would never have been done."

"They may yet vote you out of your job," Abby pointed out.

"Yeah. I was looking for a job when I found this one. I don't care."

"The next Viceroy could cancel this decree."

Rita snorted. "You just watch them try. Once the pig has a bucket of acorns, there ain't no way you're getting them acorns back. Once folks around here realize what they now own, you ain't gonna take it away from them. Not without a fight."

With that thought, Abby took her leave.

The drive back to Government House was quiet as she mulled over the twists and turns of what Granny Rita had dumped on her. As much as Abby hated to admit it, the old biddy had some good points. The truth was that the money grabbers in human space would demand, sooner or later, that they get something in return for what they'd sent here. Unfortunately, Rita's response created all kinds of complex challenges. It might cut the strings human space had on Alwa's industry, but was there anyone here on Alwa Station that could wield all the power Rita had gathered up and put into one person's hand?

Kris Longknife had managed to juggle a whole lot of things, but Kris was kind of unique, one powerful gal who could address all the challenges facing Alwa who also knew how to depend on and get the most out of the people around her.

Be that as it may be, the biggest problem of them all still was that, having let the horse out of the barn, how do you get the damn critter to come back in?

Abby had the cabby drop her back at Government House. No surprise, the people who had been there when she left were still there when she got back. She quickly filled them in on the why and wherefore of Rita's little power play.

Ada frowned. "Why am I just now hearing about some honchos from Wardhaven trying to take back our fabrication plants?"

"I'm sorry," Abby said, speaking for her boss. "They got in and Kris Longknife had them packed off to the *Wasp's* brig in just under an hour. I guess no one wanted to admit we'd dodged a bullet."

"So how come Granny Rita knew all about it?" Kuno asked.

Abby shrugged. "I have no idea how she gets her information. Do you?"

The Colonial winced.

Ada took over the conversation. "I don't care why or what, there is no way I want to have Rita sitting on all our eggs."

"I agree," Abby said, but noted that Ada hadn't said anything about it not being a good idea for any one particular person sitting on all the eggs.

Indeed, the four Colonials were exchanging glances like a couple of teenagers who'd just come up with the idea of throwing a multi-gender pajama party . . . with no pajamas in sight . . . and couldn't wait for the adult supervision to go away.

"Well, if you'll excuse me, I need to be getting back," Abby said, standing.

"The shuttle's not leaving until morning," Ada pointed out. "You can stay at my place."

"I'd rather bunk down with the shuttle crew so I don't miss them. Who knows, they might launch a bit early and I might be a bit late, what with you serving me one of those wonderful Colonial breakfasts."

"You're really missing out on a treat," sure sounded like a bribe being offered.

Abby shook her head. Lago was told to get her to the shuttle hanger. Fifteen minutes later, Abby was back at the port. She waited until Lago was out of sight before rousting out the duty shuttle crew and ordering the ready longboat for an immediate launch.

"You know, the folks around here get mighty pissed when we do a launch this late at night."

"If you don't launch when I say so, there's gonna be some people in orbit that are gonna be mightily pissed. Who do you want mad at you?"

They launched thirty minutes later.

Abby spent the flight up to Canopus Station thinking. She definitely had a problem.

Rita had recognized the basic one: how would Alwa keep the humans on the other side of the galaxy from messing in their life? Sure, they were the ones who had paid for all that nice, expensive equipment in the first place, but they'd provided it as part of a prop to cover their own ass. If the aliens conquered and plundered Alwa, they wanted the raiders to think they had beaten the system that had caused them so much grief. That way, the aliens wouldn't go looking for the real source of the people who had refused to roll over and die.

Of course, that entire concept was flawed. If the alien

raiders had any skill with DNA, one sample of flesh from a bird and one from a human would show the two were from totally different evolutionary lines.

Still, the blood and sweat of the fight that the people and birds of the Alwa system had put up the last couple of years was certainly fair exchange for the expensive heavy manufacturing fabs the corporations from human space had donated.

Rita's solution, nationalizing everything from the other side of the galaxy and reserving all its production for Alwa, was an idea that Abby expected to be acceptable to everyone.

Except it put Granny Rita in the cat bird seat, controlling everything.

And even if the Colonials voted her out of the Viceroy's job, whoever got it could be just as bad. Maybe not immediately, but power corrupts and total power corrupts totally, or whatever the wise man said.

Abby needed to come up with a way to protect the means of production here from distant finagling, while keeping some local from killing the goose that lays the golden egg.

She was still thinking about how to square that circle as she walked into Pipra's office.

"I wasn't expecting to see you until morning," Pipra said.

Abby filled her in on what she now knew about Granny Rita's little plot, then added, "If I'm reading our friends in the Colonial Government right, while they don't want Rita running the show, they ain't at all bothered by the idea of one of them being our boss."

"Damn. Once something like this gets loose, it's not going to stop and it's not going to be pretty. It's been kind of nice having a government and industry that were working together to save our necks. Now, I guess with Kris Longknife having killed a couple of hundred billion aliens, folks feel they got enough breathing space to go back to their usual game of grabbing power and running with it."

"Boss, I got some ideas about a thing or two."

"Do I want to hear about them?"

"I think you'd rather be able to say you had no idea I'd go off and do such a damn fool stunt."

"Suddenly, I really don't want to know what you're up to."

"Yeah. Now, if you don't mind, I got a couple of pots of stew to bring to a boil at just the right time. I'm going to pull in some IOUs, so if the next lunar shuttle leaves a bit early, don't be surprised."

"I don't want to know *anything*," Pipra said, and buried her nose in the nearest reader.

Abby let herself out of the office and headed for Canopus Station Yards. Within the hour, she was sharing some beers with a dozen or so folks. Good folks, the salt of the earth type folks. If you asked them, most would call themselves worker bees. Others among them got paid to supervise the worker bees.

None were in management.

They listened to what Abby had to say, then offered some suggestions of their own. The meeting broke up just short of an hour from its start. Most of them had already called some of their best friends to get together for a beer and had to hurry out.

An hour later, Abby was sweet-talking a lunar shuttle crew into giving her a fast, 2.5 gee ride to the moon. The morning shuttle left before midnight with only one passenger.

Abby spent most of the next morning trotting from meeting to meeting. She made use of the newly completed maglev train to get some face time before noon at the new complex at East crater. Her meeting with her friends at the North complex had to be by phone, but she got that moving.

She held up at her favorite bar in New Town, shared beers with whoever wanted to talk to her, and checked her mail regularly. There were a few disappointments, but nothing she couldn't live with. She checked in with Pipra to see if there was any action on the Granny Rita or Colonial Government front, but Pipra knew nothing. Happy with a day well spent, even if it wasn't in her lover's arms, Abby went to bed early.

She fell asleep composing her next move.

The next day was busy. Proposals were floated, shot down, modified, reviewed, and polished. Abby was pulling strings that stretched all over Alwa orbit. Because of the time delay, she wasn't sure that the asteroid miners would make it in, but they could sign up later.

Nine o'clock that night, Abby did one final scan down her first official transmission in her new capacity. Danged if she didn't find a typo that had survived all those reviews. She corrected it, and hit send.

Official machines from Government House to every yard in orbit and every plant on the moon began to spit out a message that caused consternation wherever it was read.

LET IT BE KNOWN THAT WE, THE AMALGAMATED UNION OF CRAFTS, FABRICATION OPERATORS, SMART METAL™ BUILDERS, AND ASSOCIATED

WORKERS AS WELL AS THE ALWA ASSOCIATION OF FIRST LINE SUPERVISORS, DO HEREBY REFUSE TO HAVE OUR WORKPLACE CONFISCATED BY THE ILLEGAL AND UNPRECEDENTED ACTIONS OF THE VICEROY FOR ALWA DOWNSIDE. WE REJECT ANY EFFORTS TO DIVERT OUR WORK FROM THE PRESENT DRIVE TO MEET THE NEEDS OF ALL PEOPLE OF THE ALWA SYSTEM AND ASSURE THEIR COMMON DEFENSE. WE DEMAND THAT THE RELATIONSHIPS OF ALL WORKERS, MANAGERS AND GOVERNMENTS OF THE ALWA SYSTEM BE RESTORED TO THEIR PREVIOUS CONDITION OF HARMONY AND PRODUCTIVITY.

ABSENT AN AGREEMENT WITHIN THE NEXT 48 HOURS TO RETURN TO THAT PREVIOUS STATE OF LABOR TRANQUILITY, WE HAVE UNANIMOUSLY AGREED TO DOWN TOOLS.

WE ARE PREPARED TO STRIKE TO PRESERVE OUR SACRED RIGHTS EARNED BY THE SWEAT OF OUR OWN BROWS.

Signed: ABIGAIL NIGHTINGALE, BUSINESS MANAGER, THE AMALGAMATED UNION OF CRAFTS, FABRICATION OPERATORS, SMART METAL™ BUILDERS AND ASSOCIATED WORKERS AND THE ALWA ASSOCIATION OF FIRST LEVEL SUPERVISORS

Abby was ready to get a good night's sleep. No doubt, tomorrow would be a busy day, but messages started coming in from all over the place before she could lay her weary body down.

"I knew I was knocking over a hornet's nest, but I figured it would take a while to hit the ground," Abby said to herself as she pulled back on her clothes and called up the lunar to Canopus Station shuttle.

"We already got orders to haul the ready shuttle out of the hanger and prep it for immediate launch, Abby. There's talk of jacking it up to 3.5 gees. Don't they know a lunar shuttle don't do nothing above two gees?"

"You tell them that it can't do more than 1.5 gees, Albert. My old bones are getting tired of all this hurry up and wait."

"I'll tell them that. We union workers got to stick together."

Abby hoped she wouldn't live to rue this day. What did Kris Longknife say way too often? "It seemed like a good idea at the time."

RUTH LONGKNIFE'S FIRST CHRISTMAS

Ruthie's first Christmas is set after Kris Longknife Bold. Every child has to have a first Christmas, but being a Longknife, Ruthie's Christmas is not at all what you'd expect.

RUTHIE LONGKNIFE'S FIRST CHRISTMAS: A SHORT STORY

Admiral Kris Longknife softy bounced little seven-month-old Ruthie Longknife on her hip, and watched the sparkle of the Christmas tree lights reflected in her daughter's bright eyes. Kris breathed deeply of the woodland scent from the freshly cut tree.

This tiny Longknife would have a real first Christmas.

Around them, two-dozen people were busy making Ruthie's first Christmas special. Jack's entire family; his dad, mom, sister, even brother, was here, helping him put ornaments on the sparkling ten-foot-tall tree.

Kris had invited her own mother and father, but they had declined due to a scheduling conflict. She winced at the reflection on how low she was on her parents' priority list.

However, Kris's brother and Member of Parliament, Honovi, was here. He'd brought his lovely wife Linda, and his three children with him. In descending order, they were Billy, seven, Goyath, five, and Brenda, three. With plenty of hugs, they were in ascending order, putting ornaments on the tree just as high as their little hands could reach.

Brenda's lower limbs were a bit disorganized but Linda

protected her daughter from her oldest child's insistence on symmetry. "You didn't do all that well four years ago when you were three and did the lowest limbs of our tree. When Brenda's busy with cookies, you can rearrange things if you insist."

Placated and hugged, seven-year-old Billy, still missing two teeth, went off to add bulbs to fill blanks at his height.

Harvey, the old chauffeur at Nuu House, was supervising the tree's decoration from a chair, an eggnog in one hand. His other hand pointed to blank spots on the tree for children and adults of various heights to fill in. The indomitable old soldier who'd been chauffeur since Ray and Rita Longknife lived in Nuu House, was starting to show his age, as unthinkable as that was to Kris.

His wife, Lotty, kept a supply of Christmas cookies, eggnog, and the adult version of eggnog, flowing smoothly from her kitchen.

All of Ruthie's nannies, some with their husbands and kids as well, were here, helping, celebrating, and enjoying themselves. There were rumors that Santa Claus might visit with presents for good little boys and girls.

For once, the living room in Nuu House looked warm and inviting.

Kris breathed it all in, and hoped this was only the first of many, many, Christmases to come.

It hadn't been this way. Not for as long as she could remember.

When she went to college and talked her folks into opening up Nuu House for her, she'd had little use for the holidays. Mostly, they meant being with Mother and Father at this or that political event. Minding herself carefully in clothes that usually were scratchy and making sure not to do anything that might lose Father a vote.

Once on her own, she did her best to avoid the hubbub. Usually she'd invite her few friends for a couple of visits to their favorite pizza parlor.

Kris had been pretty low key during college. Having been burned not once but twice by false boyfriends, she kept most people at arm's length. The few she let get close to her were themselves low drama types. A pizza for Thanksgiving or Christmas fit them all quite well.

Nuu House always had a Christmas tree, and a small one in Lotty's kitchen. If Kris felt a need for some Christmas cheer, real cheer, not political or other cheer with strings attached, she could find it there.

The Navy, of course, celebrated Christmas and a slew of other holidays that fell that time of year. Kris paid the appropriate amount of attention to what excited those around her, she was, after all, Billy Longknife's daughter. Still, none of them had ever moved her.

Now there was today. A week after Thanksgiving, Jack had taken Ruthie and Kris out to buy a tree. It had taken a small Marine detachment and Special Agent Foile's team to approve an acceptable Christmas tree lot. The lucky one was run by Girl Guides to raise money for themselves and veterans.

It had taken all the Guides' goodwill to put up with a full Longknife invasion. Kris had insisted that they schedule themselves early in the day when fewest customers would have to be held at gunpoint.

"We don't hold people at gunpoint," Jack insisted, through a grin.

They didn't, but who wanted to buy a tree when there were a dozen combat Marines in full battle rattle patrolling up and down the aisles? Kris's suggestion that they be organized into groups, decked out in Santa Claus hats, and sent up and down the rows singing Christmas carols did not go over at all well with Gunny.

Kris could only shake her head. No wonder she was such a Grinch.

Then Jack fell in love with the most beautiful . . . and tallest . . . tree on the lot. It would likely take a place like the living room at Nuu House to give that monster a home. Several Marines were dragooned into stacking rifles and lugging the tree to one of their gun trucks.

Kris couldn't help but giggle. The sight of a gun truck with a huge Christmas tree tied to its top had to be one of the strangest sights of the holidays. As luck would have it, the front gate at Nuu House was staked out by a lone paparazzi hoping to get a shot of what Christmas might be like inside.

Kris found out later from Special Agent Foile that the photographer got $50,000 for that shot. He couldn't have made more money if he'd gotten a photo of Kris at the beach coming out of the surf nude.

So, the tree arrived safe and sound, and the Longknife family survived getting it as well.

It had taken three Marines to get the tree in a secure and upright position. After this decorating party, Kris would be hosting one for her Marine detachment with mainly spiked eggnog, though there would be a bowl of plain eggnog for the underage Marines to drink from. Both would be refilled regularly.

The tree decorating party was going so very well. Ruthie couldn't take her eyes off of the tree. Kris made the mistake of letting her bright eyes get too close, and her pudgy fingers immediately snapped up a string of lights and jammed one in her mouth. Fortunately, her few teeth and jaw weren't strong enough to crack a well-protected LED light.

Several nannies rushed to the rescue with other sparkly things for Ruth to grab and put in her mouth to replace the string of lights.

Kris backed off a bit from the tree.

Jack's sister and mom asked for and got their chance to bounce Ruth and enjoy her reaction to the tree full of lights. Momma Montoya was warming to Kris. She had almost forgiven her for seducing her son away from some good Catholic girl. When the topic surfaced, Jack would insist he was not seduced, but his mom never ceased insisting it was so.

It was a kind of a running joke between Kris and Jack now. "It's close to bedtime. Can I interest you in a little bit of seduction?" It was a line either one of them could use to get a laugh and a fast trip to the bedroom.

The party went long and was enjoyed by everyone, even Ruthie, although she closed her eyes before the tree was finished and traveled off to that sweet place infants go.

The duty nanny took her up to the nursery and set the alarms. Nelly would see that Ruthie slept contented for however long she chose to. She was sleeping through the nights quite regularly now.

With the tree done, Santa Claus did appear. He was a retired chief who'd grown the most spectacular white beard in retirement, and grown his chief's belly into something truly fit for a Saint Nick. He arrived in good humor. He quickly gained acceptance from even the most doubting of six-year-olds who got to pull his beard and prove to their skeptical selves that there really was a Santa Claus.

Kris had put a significant chunk of change aside to fill up a Credit Chit and told her Secret Service agents and nannies to please select and charge to that account toys for their children, nephews, nieces, or younger cousins. They had been quite surprised by the size of the amount Kris gave each one of them.

Every child was so delighted by Santa's expert knowledge of their wishes and hopes. Even Agent Foile's teenagers got in the spirit when they found Nelly had chosen new computers for each of them. Their new computers didn't come with one of Nelly's kids, but they'd been designed by Nelly and her kids and would likely beat anything on the market.

The boys were dumbfounded.

"Kris, they've got computers better than mine!" Foile exclaimed.

"You haven't opened your Christmas presents. I think some presents may have magically appeared under the tree for you and your three favorite agents."

The nannies and the leadership of the Marine detachment also had presents. Now, all could be on Nelly Net. If Nelly or Jack's Sal monitored something Kris or Jack needed to know, it went straight to the top.

Nelly was turning into quite the command center.

That night, Kris lay in Jack's arms and stroked them. "Your family is so close. So . . . family. They hug. They have friendly good humor. Do you think we could be like that in twenty years?"

"Of course, we'll be," Jack answered without thought.

"My folks aren't like that," Kris pointed out.

"Honovi and Linda look to be well on their way to a contented family life."

Kris sighed. "I watched Linda hug, caress, and even kiss the kids. The way they showered love on each other. That was so beautiful."

Jack said nothing. He'd seen Kris around her family. She

didn't quite have to stand at attention in her father's presence, but it wasn't that far off.

"Honey," Jack said, rolling over onto an elbow and looking down at Kris. "Your brother and his wife are loving and nurturing their children. When Ruthie is three or five or seven, she'll have a mother that is just as loving and nurturing as any woman on this planet. I don't know what happened to the Longknifes between Ray and Billy, but it doesn't have to pass through you to another generation."

"It doesn't?" Kris said, tasting the words and finding them hard to swallow.

"Nope. It doesn't."

Jack held her tight until she joined Ruthie in dreamland.

Yes, Kris was enjoying Christmas this year as something warm and special.

However, there was one invitation she didn't quite know what to do with.

Grampa Al had invited everyone to his offices, what she teasingly called the Tower of Insecurity for a small family get together. Honovi told Kris that these were usually ignored by both him and Father. Kris, however, was being attacked by the spirit of Christmas cheer. Or maybe the eggnog. Or it might have been Ruthie's snaggletooth grin.

"I think we ought to go," Kris told her older brother. "My Ruthie, your three kids, how often has Grampa Al gotten a chance to see them? It's Christmas, Brother. He's offered us his hand. I'm in favor of taking it."

"You sure he won't hold us all hostage for some profitable business proposal he wants or a law he needs passed?"

Kris almost swatted her brother, which was hard to do over the net. She won, of course, in the end, and Honovi brought their father around. Their visit was set for the week before Christmas.

It was a good thing they allowed plenty of time. After much coordination between security detachments, that went long and convoluted, it was all decided. Kris's convoy would be merged into Honovi's. Then, they would all merge into the Prime Minister's motorcade.

"We're going to make a mess of traffic," Honovi pointed out.

"It should clear out by rush hour," Kris insisted. "Besides, most people are taking time off. So long as we don't go near a mall and mess up their traffic flow, we shouldn't lose Father too many votes."

Thus, it happened, that Kris found herself, Ruthie, Jack and a whole lot of her family with several small armies of security details surrounding them driving into the basement of Grampa Al's Tower of Insecurity.

It was interesting to watch Honovi's kids in this tight security bubble with big gruff men everywhere to be seen. The two older boys stayed close to Dad, often holding his hand, never getting more than a few feet from him. They showed no concern about the busy adults bustling about them. Neither did they show any fear.

Clearly, the kids had been trained not to be concerned and at the same time not to wander off when strong men armed were hemming them in.

Little Brenda, at three, watched everything with wide eyes from her mother's arms. Clearly, she'd seen this rodeo before. Clearly, she did not like it. However, with mommy's arms around her, she was willing to tolerate this without complaint.

With luck, this would be Ruthie in the years to come. Aware of her security bubble, but going on about her life within it, just as her mom and dad did.

As Kris was watching Honovi's kids, she spotted the guard stations she, Jack, and Penny, had been assigned to when they made their failed effort to scale the tower uninvited for a small tête-à-tête with Grampa Al. She somehow doubted they'd get a tour of the space shuttle she'd used to get out of that mess and straight into another.

"That's where we started our little assault on Grampa Al's tower," Kris told Ruthie.

Honovi's two oldest kids were fascinated that their Aunt Krissie had broken through Grampa Al's security perimeter. Grandmother Brenda was rather scandalized.

"Do you really want to put ideas in these children's heads?"

"Mom, they're Longknifes," Kris said. "They need to know what that means. I was rather dumbfounded the first time anyone tried to kill me. It took me several failed assassinations before I realized they were no accident. Forewarned is forearmed."

Honovi's kids watched Kris in fascination, then they turned to Gramama to return the shot.

"Not all Longknifes go around dodging assassins. Kris, you would do well to stay home and then they'd never come after you."

Kris looked at Honovi, then at the rather large armies of security details surrounding them.

"Mother," Honovi said, "the last assassination attempt against you, me, or Dad, was last week. Our security is good. Better than good."

Mother looked to Father. He shrugged. "Sorry, Brenda, but your son is correct. They happen. They fail. We ignore them. I did make a mistake assuming that allowing Kris to join the Navy would move her into a secure environment. It turned out not to be so. Sorry, darling. Honovi, I'm not at all bothered by Kris telling your children stories. However, I do think you might want to talk to the children when you get home, and maybe sleep with the nursery door open tonight."

Honovi nodded in agreement.

About that time, the security bubble moved out. Each primary and their team took a different elevator direct to the fiftieth floor where they were asked to hold in a side room. After five minutes, Kris turned to Special Agent Foile and just raised an eyebrow.

He spoke into his cuff for a moment, then frowned.

THEY SEEM TO BE HAVING AN INFESTATON OF NANOS. MOST OF WHAT THEY ARE FINDING ARE SCOUTS, BUT A FEW HAVE EXPLOSIVES ABOARD. THEY ARE TAKING A BIT LONGER THAN EXPECTED TO CLEAN THIS ROOM

NELLY? Kris asked.

THE NANOS ARE LAST YEAR'S TECH OR OLDER, SO IT IS JUST A MATTER OF ELIMINATING THEM. I AM REVIEWING THE SITUATION. I'LL TELL YOU IF I THINK YOU NEED TO BE MORE CONCERNED.

Three minutes later, they were invited to take the next bank of elevators up to the one hundredth floor. They were now divided into two different elevators. Honovi and his brood on one with their security team. Kris's team was reduced to barely more than Special Agent Foile and three of his best as she was added to her father's elevator full of his Secret Service agents.

As the ride began, Nelly said, "WE HAVE A BATTALION OF DEFENSIVE NANOS ABOARD OUR

ELEVATOR CAR. THEY ARE TRYING TO ELIMINATE THE BOTS AND NANOS THAT ARE STILL WITH US OR GOT IN WITH IS. I NOTE THAT THE ELEVATOR IS NOT MOVING AT ITS MOST EFFICIENT SPEED. I SUSPECT THEY ARE USING THE TIME TO DESTROY INVADERS."

As they rose, the seconds were punctuated by small pops and sparkles in the air. Kris put the blanket over Ruthie's baby bucket, but Nelly did better, converting the transport bucket into a survival pod with its own air filter. There were advantages to having a baby bassinet made by a supercomputer out of Smart Metal™.

Ruth was the safest person in the whole tower.

So, Ruthie missed out when Kris said. "Dad, how did Grampa Al get his hands on Sarin gas?"

"Sarin gas?" Mother asked. "What is Sarin gas?"

"Nothing, love. Kris, I really wish you wouldn't say things that disturb your mother," Dad said, not answering the question. Not at all.

Kris exchanged glances with Jack then her father then back to Jack.

IF YOU'RE TELLING ME 'LET'S YOU AND HIM FIGHT', I'M NOT GOING TO DO IT, Jack answered on Nelly Net. YOU GET HIM TO ANSWER YOUR OWN QUESTION OF IT AIN'T GONNA GET ANSWERED."

Kris's question went unanswered

They finally reached the hundredth floor and it was time to change elevators again. This time, they were held in the vestibule of the elevator they'd just ridden up as defensive nanos scoured them. Security personnel in black suits, ear plugs and all, went over them with wands, not once, but three times.

"This must be a very stubborn nano infestation," Special

Agent Foile said to one of the fellows overseeing the pat down.

He said nothing.

I WON'T BE SURPRISED IF SOME OF THESE NANOS DON'T GET ALL THE WAY TO AL'S OFFICE, Nelly said to all on Nelly Net. THE NUMBER OF SLEEPER NANOS ON YOU IS DRIVING THEM CRAZY. I BELIEVE THEY HAVE SUGGESTED TO THEIR SUPERIORS THAT WE BE RETURNED TO THE BASEMENT, FORCE TO STRIP NAKED, AND SHOWER. THESE ARE NOT OPTIONS THEIR BOSS WANTS TO SUGGEST TO THEIR EMPLOYER.

They were finally allowed to move around to the next bank of elevators. Once again, they rose slowly. In fact, they slowed down even more as they passed the 125th floor. Nelly told them, but Kris was able to feel it herself.

They stopped at the 150th, were allowed to change to the fourth bank of elevators and again slowly climbed to the very top, 200th floor of the tower. Kris knew from experience that the top most floor was reserved for offices. Grampa Al had his personal suites on the two floors down from there.

SO, THIS IS A BUSINESS MEETING.

KRIS, HE COULD BE WORKING UNTIL WE GET THERE.

EITHER WAY, JACK, IT DOESN'T BODE WELL.

OF THAT, WE CAN AGREE

The elevator opened on a huge expanse of carpet. Here, three secretaries at three different desks widely spaced around the vast plain of royal blue carpeting waited patiently for anything to happen. Since all three looked like graduates of Wardhaven special forces, Kris doubted that typing was their main concern.

Kris and Honovi led the way to the middle secretary.

They had experience with taking their children to visit their grandfather.

Billy Longknife had not talked to his father for nearly twenty years. The two had not exchanged a word since Al had demanded that his son withdraw from politics after the death of little Eddy.

From the way he hung back, it was quite possible that he was prepared to go another twenty.

The one thing Kris noticed was the total lack of Christmas cheer in the waiting area. There were several visual bits of art that Kris strongly suspected were holograms, but there wasn't a holotree anywhere.

This time, the secretary did not attempt to slow them down. He was up and out of his chair, buttoning his suit jacket to hide his automatic, and leading them to the door to Al's office. Kris and Honovi paused there for a moment while their security details and the Prime Ministers did a quick check to verify that the reputedly most safe place on Wardhaven was, indeed, safe and up to government standards. Done, they withdrew to wait just outside the office door.

Only the Longknifes entered to meet with the man they all descended from.

From the smell of it, Grampa Al had splurged on a real tree. It was fully decorated and sparkling with lights next to a conversational pit. Once Honovi's kids spotted the presents under the tree, their best behavior vanished.

The boys dropped their dad's hands and Brenda wiggled out of her mom's arms. Together, they bolted right past Grampa Al and didn't stop until they were kneeling in front of the tree, excitedly reporting that some of the fancy wrapped boxes had their names on them.

"Can we open them?" "Can we, please?" "Oh, please,

please!" was the youngest and cutest. She had a bit of a lisp at present.

"Ask your great-grandfather," Honovi said, which led to a second round of begging.

Al had ignored the children, being busy asking the adults what they wanted to drink. "You may, in a little while. If you are good."

So, three kids settled on their knees by the Christmas tree, being very good and very silent, but making sure the tree and its presents didn't make a dash for the door.

Mentally, Kris shook her head. Al had ignored these tiny Longknifes only to play his power games with them when they begged for his attention.

This ends. This ends here. All this cold bullshit ends with my generation.

I don't know where it came from, but I will nourish my children. This will not pass it to Ruthie and I so hope Honovi and Linda are as successful as they seem to be.

But to all who looked her way, Kris wore a smile as Al insisted on serving all the adults a drink of their choice. It was three o'clock, but Billy actually talked to his father as he ordered a scotch and Brenda a daiquiri. Honovi and his wife asked for white wine and Al produced it with a flair. Kris and Jack asked for and were served Chamomile tea with a bit of a scowl from their host.

While Alexander proved himself the congenial host, the three couples settled onto the three available couches. Beside Kris, Ruthie's baby bucket became a small bassinet under Nelly's quick and easy control.

So naturally, Ruthie announced she wanted up. As soon as Kris had her in her arms, the cantankerous infant wanted down. Kris set the smallest princess on the carpet.

"Is she crawling yet?" Linda asked.

"No," Kris said. "She's got this other thing she does." And as they watched, Ruthie did it.

Her pudgy hand and legs waved about but never quite touched the carpet. Her milk belly kept her quite high and it looked impossible for her to go anywhere. Still, she giggled and cooed and wiggled and before anyone realized it, she was over next to the couch with Honovi and his wife.

"Did anyone see how she did that?" Kris asked.

Brenda went to pick Ruthie up, but the infant quickly objected to her grandmother's attention and Kris relieved her mother of a fussy infant. She held Ruth until she decided she'd seen enough and closed her eyes and fell asleep. Kris laid her carefully in her bassinet and laid a blanket over her. She sucked happily in her dreams.

Only when Grampa Al was satisfied that everyone had a drink did he settle down in his big chair and smile at them, "I am so glad to see all of you here," he said. "We don't get together nearly enough as a family."

He got six nods, but not a word in answer.

"So, I hope you will stay for supper. I've had my cook prepare a Christmas goose and black pudding according to an old recipe from Earth."

"That sounds delicious," Linda said, desperately trying to fill the void.

Nothing followed that.

"Can you stay for dinner?" Alexander finally asked.

"I think we can," Kris said, glancing toward Honovi.

"I'm not sure I can trust my little pixies at a fully dressed dinner table. Little Bill is not yet out of his hot dog phase, and tiny Brenda is more likely to want cheese than anything else."

"I am aware that *children* often do not perform to expectations," seemed to hint that the three carpet rats around the tree might not be the only humans unable to perform to expectations.

"I had my cook prepare a small table in the kitchen. I thought the three youngsters could eat in there. Likely they'll also want to play with their new toys."

"That might work out very well," Linda said, glancing at her husband. "Won't it, honey?"

"Yes, I think so," Honovi allowed.

While this strained conversation was going on, Kris had been hearing a strange hum in the background. It grew louder and louder, until even Al was looking for it. "What in God's seven hells is that racket?"

"Nanos are hurling themselves at the window," Nelly reported. "They have taken off the aluminum reflective coating and are now starting to abrade the glass."

"That is three inch, bulletproof glass," Grampa Al said, not rising from his chair, totally secure in his Tower of Security.

"The nanos are under some control," Nelly said. "They are also attacking the steel holding the glass panes in. I think they are making more progress there and reinforcing the attack.

"Computer, inform me what is being done to defend the windows of my office," Al demanded.

"Nothing, sir."

"Why forever not?"

"There is not an attack on your office windows, sir."

"Computer, get me Security Central."

A moment later Al continued. "There is a God awful noise outside my office window. I am informed that they are under attack by nanos. Confirm or determine the error of this report."

"Nanos outside the 200th floor, sir?"

"Yes."

"We don't have anything that goes that high."

"Well, get someone on the roof and report what they see. Now! What do I pay you for?"

"Yes, sir. Immediately, sir."

"Nelly, can you repulse a nano attack?" Kris asked.

"With what, Kris? Alexander Longknife, do you have any Smart Metal at hand that I could convert into nano defenders?"

"Of course, not! Why would I have Smart Metal up here?" said the man who owned the patent on the stuff.

"To save your life, sir," Nelly growled, clearly wanting to replace the sir with something else.

Kris was already reaching for Ruthie. "Take the bassinet," Kris ordered.

Even as Kris lifted Ruthie into her arms, the bassinet began to erode away as it evaporated into millions of defensive nanos.

"I will form a defense bubble around you, but you need to get in close," Nelly said.

"Children. Here. Now," Honovi commanded.

It told well of their upbringing that the children abandoned the shiny packages and ran to their father and mother. The boys took their father's hand. Brenda was pulled up by her mother. Around Kris, her family closed in on each other. For the first time in a very long time, Kris found herself touching her mother and father. Honovi and Linda stepped in close to Kris and Jack. Only Al remained in his chair, sipping his scotch.

"This is preposterous. There is nothing to fear."

"Sir," came from Al's computer assistant. "We sent several men up to the roof. They were attacked. Two were killed. More nanos got in the building before we could slam the door. Some of the attackers are micro bots and carry explosives. We will release all our defensive nanos. That should defeat this attack."

"There is a great distance between should and will," Kris said. "Grampa Al, get over here."

This time the man came.

"Nelly, can you hold?"

"I do not know, Kris. I may need your help," and suddenly Kris saw the room in a totally different perspective.

She and Jack with their two powerful computers were the central node in a series of nodes that spread out from them. She could not make out all the tiny nanos at the end of all the nodes, but she knew they were there, the same as she knew her fingernails were at the end of her hand.

"Can we fight and beat them here?" Kris asked. "Should we retreat into the central office and get everyone on the floor into this bubble?"

"The windows will not hold long," Nelly said. "My scouts already report attack bots and attacking nanos in the office space. I agree Kris, we could better protect all the humans here from a redoubt in the center of the office."

"Folks, we are going to walk slowly, and carefully, everyone hand in hand, until we get to the waiting room," Kris ordered. "Al, get your minions to report to your secretary's desk."

"I will not..."

"Do it now or they die," Wardhaven's premier fighting commander ordered.

Her grandfather meekly told his computer to call his people out of their offices and to his secretary's desk. Meek was a strange thing to see on Alexander Longknife.

"Jack, you cover the rear, please," Kris said as she, with

Ruthie in arms, led her family toward the door. Once there, Billy stepped ahead to open it for Kris, then waited as his family filed out, going through only a step ahead of Jack.

"Should I close the door or leave it open?" Jack asked.

"Keep it open," Nelly ordered. "It's not going to hold back anything that can break through those windows and I need to be able to move my nanos."

Outside was chaos. Several bodies lay dead across the vast expanse of the waiting room. The three truncated Longknife security teams had their weapons drawn and had formed a circle, weapons out, but there was little they could do. Mahomet had his black box out, so at least the teams knew what they faced, but their weapons were worthless.

Kris took her family into the circle the security people had formed, then organized her defensive perimeter with Jack.

Now two dozen men and women in business suits hurried from offices toward the central desk. Several of them did not make it. There was no pattern to who fell, or where or why. Death came randomly.

Kris moved her family and security team at a slow walk toward that desk. There, she told everyone to sit down in as tight a space as they could manage. She sat on the desk with Ruthie in her arms and her back to Jack. They were in both the most protected place on the 200th floor, and, at the same time, the center that if it fell, the entire leadership of Nuu Enterprises, as well as the prime minister of Wardhaven, died.

"Can't we take the elevator down?" Grampa Al demanded.

"How easy is it to cut a wire?" Kris answered, then quickly added, "Nelly, patch me through to the Security Center."

"Who is this?" came quickly.

"This is Admiral Kris Longknife, I command a redoubt on the 200th floor. I am defending your boss and his entire family from a hostile nano attack. Now, listen to me. Evacuate the building. Do not use the elevators. Understood?"

"Yes, Admiral."

"I need Smart Metal up here, soonest. Get me some and send it up the elevators."

"We don't have any, ma'am."

"Then get some. Your boss's life depends on it. Move. Now!"

"Yes, ma'am."

Kris hoped that he could do something. Ruthie's bassinet had formed a limited number of nanos. Around her neck, Kris felt the simulated diamond necklace that held Nelly begin to melt away to the minimum needed to hold her in place at Kris's collar bone. Likewise, Jack's tie tack began to shrink, contributing all it had to Nelly's defensive nanos

Nelly was calling in her last reserves.

There was a whoosh of air through the floor as a glass pane fell away from the face of the building. In Kris's mind's eye, she could see as Nelly pulled back her defensive perimeter to just those around her.

Now, several waves of defense nanos stormed forward to meet the invaders in Al's office. There, they fought. The big attack bots were easy to spot, even to the naked eye. They looked like little more than flies, or gnats. Nelly's nanos attacked them, stripped them of their wings and sent them crashing down.

But not all bots died easily. They began to explode as soon as they lost their wings, taking their attacking nanos with them.

Kris ordered a change in her own nanos attack. Now they weakened a wing root. The bots flew on, then lose their wing a few centimeters later where their explosion hurt nothing.

Kris didn't actually make the decision for her nanos to do things differently. Her thoughts solved problems at the speed of light, and her orders went out at the same speed.

Was this what it was to be Nelly?

Somewhere another window went down, or maybe the door up to the roof gave way. Suddenly, a wave of attackers hit them from the stairwell.

Kris peeled as many nanos as she could from the defense perimeter around those she loved and sent them hurtling out to give battle to this new onslaught. She pulled nanos back from Al's office to reinforce her defenses, then sent more nanos to fight in the space between the central desk and the elevator and stairwell.

The fight went long and hard. Nelly's nanos were far superior to the attackers, but the swarm attack took its toll. Kris finally had to order all her remaining nanos back to the defense perimeter. There were just not enough left for a defense in depth.

Now they were surrounded by attacking nanos and micro bots. Held back from the humans, the nanos and bots changed their attack mode. Some began picking away at the ceiling tiles above them and brought them crashing down. The tiles were made of foam and fiber and weighed nothing so they did no real harm to the humans.

However, some of boards trapped defending nanos under them. Nelly became more careful and now usually pulled her forces back before a tile fell.

The enemy was taking out more of its own nanos and micro bots with tiles than any of Nelly's.

Still, Kris had only so many nanos and the attacker seemed to never run out.

Then an elevator dinged and its door opened. Inside was a bit of art. An ugly statue of something. Kris wasn't at all sure what. What mattered to her was that it was made of dumb metal.

Dumb metal was very much like Smart Metal™ with one key exception. It could only be reworked twice. After that, it just disintegrated into a puddle of shiny goo. That particular exception had once almost killed Kris.

Now Kris was very grateful for the stuff.

Nelly took control of the programmable matter and gave it the last shape it could ever take. Nanos streamed off the piece of art and began attacking the nanos and bots from the rear.

Now, some of Nelly's nanos merged to form micro bots of her own. They slipped past the line of attack nanos flowing into the line and followed them to their source.

Four minutes later, Nelly had a picture of several trucks parked three blocks from the entrance to the Al Longknife business complex.

Jack had ordered a platoon of their Marines out of Nuu House the moment it became clear they were under attack. They were two minutes out, and were only too happy to be re-tasked with hitting that launch site.

While Kris and Nelly continued the battle around their loved ones, now going much better thanks to the dumb metal reinforcements, Jack and Sal took over the counter attack.

The Marines and their gun trucks raced through the streets, looking for all the world like they would charge down the street into the Longknife office park. The attackers' base was totally unprepared when the Marine trucks slammed on the brakes, skidded into a turn and gunned down their street; half from one direction, half from the other.

The assault team had their hands up before the Marines dismounted. Jack had nanos searching the launch site. He knew exactly what machines needed destroying. The first Marines into each truck emptied a clip into a shiny gray box with lots of dials.

Around Kris, the attacking nanos and bots lost all control. They flew in straight lines and crashed into walls. They flew in circles and Kris's nanos clipped their wings. They lost all interest in doing anyone any damage.

"The attack is falling apart," Kris said aloud.

"We have all the culprits in our control," Jack reported. "Two of them are babbling like mad men about who paid them to do this. Al, I think one of your competitors may be going to jail."

"He almost killed me! Killed my son, my grandchildren and my great-grandchildren. My entire family," Al said, his eyes wide, seeing nothing. Then he collapsed.

"We need a doctor here," Kris ordered on the security net as he grabbed for Al. "Al Longknife is in medical distress."

Five minutes later, a major medical reaction team raced out of the elevator. They had Al on a diagnostic bed in half a minute, and had a diagnosis of shock and a possible series of mini-strokes. They were already treating him as they rushed him toward the elevator.

Most of Al's people milled around, if not in shock, certainly bereft of direction.

Kris gave no orders. She'd used up her order book for at least a week.

"Well," Billy said, looking around. "I wonder if that

Christmas goose is still warm? Anyone here know where the dining room is?"

The secretary did indeed know where his boss ate his formal meals. He led the rest of the Longknifes down a wide flight of stairs into the living quarters. There was indeed a cook prepared to feed them. Despite his boss being absent, he was most willing to serve them.

The secretary excused himself and returned a few minutes later with all the presents for the Longknife children. Honovi's kids squealed with glee.

Ruth just wanted a breast to nibble on. She was getting breast milk less and less, but just then, Kris needed it as much as Ruthie. She found a chair that rocked and settled into it. She dropped her top and began nursing her infant.

The other three kids quickly opened their presents, to find some very expensive toys that they weren't all that excited about. What seven-year-old wants a train set? How many seven-year-olds even know what a steam locomotive was?

Honovi's youngest, who was more interested in the ripping into packaging than what was inside it, was only too happy to open all Ruthie's presents. They included a silver spoon, a golden rattle, and a silver brush with the softest of bristles to brush a baby's hair.

All were engraved with Ruth's full name, including Longknife-Montoya. On some of them, it took several lines to get the whole name down.

As dinner finished, Nelly announced, "Grampa Al is sedated and doing fine in the clinic on the 149th floor. He's asleep so we probably shouldn't visit."

So, Ruthie's very first Christmas visit with her Grampa Al proved to be very survivable, as was also her second assassination attempt.

Kris could only shake her head. Now she was having to survive assassination attempts on other Longknife lives. It didn't seem possible that living here, at home, nowhere near a warship or space station that she would still have to be ever on alert, ready to dodge incoming fire every moment of the day or night.

"Poor Ruthie. You were born a Longknife. May you ever be fast on your feet and quick with a counter attack. Merry Christmas, little one. May you have many, many more. All of them survivable."

KRIS LONGKNIFE AMONG THE KICKING BIRDS

Kicking Birds takes place during Kris Longknife Unrelenting. The book went extremely long and something had to be cut. Int he book, these events are covered by a single paragraph. If you want to know what was behind that paragraph, you'll really enjoy Kris trying to make her way through the land mines of a totally different bird culture.

1

"If I wake you up, will you hit me up side the head?" brought Kris Longknife back to wakefulness.

Without opening her eyes, Kris took stock of her situation.

Pregnant. *Check.*

Exhausted. *Check.*

Tummy upset. *Check.*

Want to roll over and go back to sleep? *You bet.*

"Consider yourself hit up side the head," Kris managed to croak at Abby.

"I got some milk. Even got a straw so you won't have to get your head up."

Kris sipped cool milk that quickly coated her queasy stomach.

"Do I smell something heavenly?"

"Fresh ginger cookies," Abby reported. "Cookie's hired himself an Ostrich for a table boy who's doing double duty as a runner."

"He knows it's life or death if I don't get my cookies," Kris said, reaching for one and nibbling at it. It was warm, chewy, and delicious. Just what her tummy wanted.

"I have to get up," was more a question than an order.

"Sorry, Baby Ducks, but you're the only one that can negotiate land use permits with the locals, or so you insist. Jack's plane is two hours out of the guano mine. You're due to meet him there, then go puddle jumping all over the veldt to make the acquaintance of some really kicky birds. You want me to come along?"

"You thinking my ass might need saving today?"

"Kind of. Also, Pipra thinks I'd be the most acceptable person from her staff to look out for their interests while you're pulling this particular miracle out of your hat."

"So, you'll serve two masters, huh?"

"Saving your neck is always job one," Abby assured Kris.

"Be sure to wear your spider silks."

"Already got them on."

Three hours later, two longboats loaded with Marines, Abby, Amanda and Jacques and a dozen Ostriches were on final approach. Parked off on the apron waiting was a large, four engine transport. The Marines' three gun rigs and one armored gun truck drove off the longboats and right into the transport.

Kris took a walk across the apron to a welcoming committee made up of Jack and the former Navy frigate skipper who now oversaw the shit farm for his crimes.

"We have a minor problem here, Kris," Jack said, still bandaged and wrapped but offering Kris a pinky finger for a hug.

"And my new problem is . . .?" Kris said, hugging the one finger.

"Sampson and Mugeridge began a hunger strike yesterday," the mine manager said, naming the two officers responsible for Kris's present uncomfortable condition as well as the child under her heart.

"I don't know how they found out that ships were headed back to human space, but they did and quickly declared themselves on a hunger strike until and unless they get a ride home."

Kris suspected that the scowl on her face was at least as bad as Jack's. Kris shook her head. "There may be a lottery for a few slots open for that run, but those two will not have their names in the hat."

"I'll pass that along to them," the former Navy officer said.

"Would you like to get your name in the lottery?" Jack asked.

"No, sir," he answered immediately. "All by myself I screwed up the best job a man can have, skipper of my own ship. It's hard to believe I was that stupid. Anyway, no. I'm doing good work here. Truth is, I'm hoping that you might find a garbage scow you need a skipper for," he said, nodding toward Kris. "I know I don't deserve it, but maybe the next time you have to put a sub under the ice of that moon to shoot Hellburners at base ships, you'll consider me."

"That was damn near a suicide mission," Jack pointed out.

"I doubt I'll get a better command," the ex-skipper admitted.

"Keep your nose clean and stay squared away and I'll think about that," Kris allowed.

"Thank you, Admiral. Now, about my two problem children?"

"Any idea how they learned what was happening up on Cannopus Station?"

"No ma'am, and that bothers me. We don't get a lot of news here. What with our long work day, we could care less about anything not at the end of our noses. I admit that them knowing what I didn't does make me wonder where the grapevine is."

"Find out," Kris said. Maybe she did have more troubles on the *Constellation* than she wanted.

"And about the two?"

"Tell them they've still got to produce their work quota. If they die, they can rest assure no one will bother to read their obit here. There's no media to carry it. Work and eat. Don't eat, they still work."

The former officer grinned. "My thoughts exactly."

"The plane is loaded, Kris. We're burning daylight," Jack pointed out.

They jogged toward their plane. It was taxiing out to the runway as they belted in. Once airborne, Kris went forward to the flight deck to get a better view of this land she was dickering for.

They were flying up a broad river that slowly meandered through a land flatter than any Kris had ever seen. In some places, the river opened up into vast marshes. The flood plain went on forever as it slowly rose to bluffs miles away on both sides of the main course. Trees dotted the land as it rolled away in breaks that led to uplands where a sea of grass covered rolling hills that went on as far as the eye could see.

But what roved that grassland was mind boggling.

Herds of four-legged critters of every size and shape, from small and fast to huge and ponderous. Here were more of the things the colonials called elephants, but even bigger.

"Do you have any idea where we're going?" Kris asked the pilot.

"I've got a pretty good idea. I'm told this is the time of year for great gatherings among the Ostriches. The orbital take has identified two large tribes, one on each side of the river. I'm headed for the larger of them."

"Can you land down there?"

"I took your man Jacques to visit a lot of these folks a bit ago. I didn't wreck the plane then. I suspect I can manage now. We got nanos to take the measure of any landing strip I think is too risky, ma'am."

"I apologize for asking," Kris said.

YOU SHOULD HAVE ASKED ME, KRIS, I COULD HAVE TOLD YOU

YOU'RE RIGHT, NELLY. I'LL TRY AND KEEP MY FOOT OUT OF MY MOUTH BY ASKING YOU NEXT TIME.

They continued to fly up-river, but now the plane was bearing toward the left-hand bank of the river. Finally, the pilot banked into a turn that had Kris tightly gripping the handholds on the overhead.

A couple of minutes of flying over the sea of grass, dotted with tree lines that marked small streams or a medium size river, and the pilot said, "I think we've got our first tribe." He pointed at widely spread out groupings of grass huts along a river valley just coming up ahead of them.

Kris went back to her seat and left the pilots to go about their business.

2

The village was too close to a small watercourse and its trees and marches; the big transport settled down several klicks away, leaving a long trail behind it of crushed grass that stood at least a meter high around them.

The Marines mounted up and drove their three light, six-wheel drive gun rigs off the cargo deck. Kris and her team, with five Ostriches, drove out last in the armored gun truck.

Five more Ostriches were from the tribes on the other side of the river. They stayed in the plane. Kris had noted half the Ostriches sat on one side of the plane, surrounded by Marines, and the other five sat on the other, equally under guard.

I COULD HAVE TOLD YOU, KRIS.

I DIDN'T MAKE A FOOL OF MYSELF, SO THAT WAS SOMETHING I DIDN'T NEED TO KNOW.

YOU HUMANS ARE NOT NEARLY CURIOUS ENOUGH.

WE HUMANS HAVE OUR LIMITS. WE LEARN TO

LIVE WITH THEM.

Enough said, Kris stood in her gun truck, trying to see everything at once.

She needed to.

There were a whole lot of things to see. Herds of herbivores dotted the land around them. Most looked more interested in chewing grass. There was an exception.

One beastie thing wasn't quite as large as the so-called elephant, but it made up for its lack of size by having three tusks on its nose, each bigger than the next.

And a nasty disposition.

One male took a dislike to these new intruders. First it got several females and young running away, then it turned and trotted toward the lead Marine gun rig.

They could have blown it apart with the main chain gun on the rig, but one Marine leveled one of the hunting rifles they'd made for the locals as the Marine rigs came to a halt.

The three-horned nightmare stopped for a moment. Then it bellowed rage and charged.

The Marine fired once. Kris would have sworn he hit the thing, but it kept coming. He worked the bolt and fired again. Then a third time.

Only then did the monster rumble to a halt. It bellowed a second time, blood flowing from its mouth. Even then, it stumbled forward. The Marine took a fourth shot.

The huge thing keeled over, bellowed once more, then breathed its last.

The Marines formed a security perimeter, and Kris went forward to examine the thing.

Even dead and on its side, it was as tall as her. "Good Lord," was all Kris could find words to say.

The five Ostriches were delighted. They bit large chunks

of meat off the mountain of flesh. "Good eats. Good eats even if dead," one told Kris.

"Is there any way we can get this dinner to the village?" Kris asked Gunny.

One of the gun rigs backed up to the carcass. A tow chain was wrapped around its three horns. A moment later a bar of Smart Metal ™ was converted into a sled. The beast was pulled onto it and everything attached to the gun rig.

Minutes later, they were on their way, only now, the Ostriches insisted on running along beside the meat. Occasionally one of them would take a bite out of it and chew the bloody mess.

"No accounting for taste," a Marine was heard to mutter.

They rolled over a low hill and down into a shallow valley. In the middle distance, a river clad in green growth meandered along. Beside it, spread a large collection of grass and reed huts. "This is a lot larger than any of the villages I visited," Jacques told Kris. "I think you may have a spot of luck."

"I could use some. What kind of luck might I finally be having?"

"I think this is a gathering of tribes. It happens every spring. They get together to have races and other contests. Women look for husbands, that kind of stuff. Any disagreements among the different tribes are settled. Usually by some kind of physical contest that likely won't result in someone becoming dead."

"Likely."

"You can never tell when these birds go at each other."

"Gee thanks, oh mighty guesser about strange customs," Kris said, dryly.

"Coming from a Longknife, I'll take that as high praise," Jacque answered through a chuckle.

The four Marine vehicles drove slowly into the valley. Two Marines gun rigs led the way, including the one towing the dead three-horned beast. Kris in her gun truck followed with one rig pulling up the rear. They cautiously approached the central village of the many stretched out along the river.

The five Ostriches running alongside dinner were joined by many others taking bites as well.

"I think they're praising your gift, Kris," Nelly said. "Either that, or the tastiness of the chow."

"I think it's the gift," Jacques said. "At least, it would be a gift if they were getting it from a hunter of their own."

They came to a clearing and the four rigs halted. In front of four of the largest huts in the villages were poles with different animal skulls on them. None were very large. If Kris stripped the skull of her kill and called it her totem, she'd outweigh all of them combined.

"Two of those totems are like gazelle and zebra. The other two are critters that root in the ground and have nasty attitudes."

"And I am big horned meanie that stomps things," Kris said. "I hope that's a good opening."

It seemed so. Lots of Ostriches, several with the fewer, but longer feathers of elders, gathered around the meat and joined in chomping off bites and praising its taste. Others were bumping chests with the five returning workers from the space station.

"Most questions seem to center on why they're back," Nelly said. "Everyone knows they signed a half year contract. They're telling anyone listening that they brought the sky walkers home to talk about a range for the sky walkers to feed on. Yes, I think I got that. They say everyone can eat as well as this everyday if the sky walkers are around."

"Are they doing our bargaining for us?" Kris asked Jacques.

"Not so much bargaining as laying the ground work, I'd say. Oh, that's what was in the duffle bags."

One of the returning workers pulled a rifle from a bag he'd left in Kris's rig. Soon the others had drawn like weapons. They looked like Colonial rifles but had a much longer stock to get it against the big bird's shoulder. The sights were on the far side of the gun, not along the top. This allowed them to fold their long necks over the top and still get a solid sight picture. The trigger was well up toward the middle of the rifle, although the bolt action was further back.

The Ostrich would have to take the weapon out of his shoulder lock to work the action. It would be a slow process until they got semi-automatic rifles.

That told Kris that an Ostrich or Rooster could not have been yesterday's assassin. She was busy just now; she'd have to mention this later to the general she had investigating that bit of misbehavior.

No surprise, the rifles were a great hit among the Ostriches.

"Kris, they want to go hunting. I foresee a problem, though, if they do," Jacques said.

"If they hunt out the area around here, they'll have to move camp sooner, right?"

"Right."

"Gunny," Kris shouted.

"Admiral."

"Hold one gun rig here with half your troop. Have the gun rigs go hunting with our five and as many of the other hunters as you can cram into the three rigs. Go at least ten miles out before you shoot anything."

Gunny's, "Aye, aye, ma'am," was neutral. Apparently, this was no great idea, but not one of her worst.

Jacques went to tell the returning hunters what Kris was offering, and soon four of them piled into the three rigs with others hanging off every hand-hold available and riding on the hood as well.

The fifth yard worker, rifle in hand, came to stand beside Kris as four groups of elders strode out to meet with her in front of the gun truck.

"My egg warmer is the mightiest hunter of the plains. He is meeting now with the strong hunters. They make a hand of fast walking people."

THAT'S TRIBES, Jacques provided on Nelly net.

"He whose path I follow with many others would have words with you," the worker Ostrich said. "He would see what you want all to see. You may speak true words now to him."

The four groups squatted down, quietly eyeing Kris.

Kris squatted down, too. When she spoke, it was eye to eye.

"I am the hunter who leads hunters among the stars," she began and quickly took them through the space battles she'd fought with "those who will stomp all heads. All eggs. Even walk off with the air you breathe."

That caused an uproar.

It only ended when the Ostrich who had come home proclaimed that he too had fought this enemy. He had worked among many to shoot a laser on one of Kris's ships.

It took a while to explain that, but when he finished, the others were back squatting and eyeing Kris.

Kris then took up the tale, describing the gifts that came

to those who worked for the sky walkers. The rifles were already in evidence. Marines behind Kris started showing pots and pans for cooking meat and knives for butchering it. Kris tried to explain that cooked meat fed more people. That got blank stares.

When the Marines brought out communication gear and TVs, things got more interesting. Kris had several of the elders talk to Ostriches in the hunting parties that had left earlier. They bragged about hunting plenty of good meat.

There were a few remarks about eating dead meat, but there were also plenty more in favor of eating a hearty meal that the old and young didn't have to run after.

Off in a corner, Kris watched as a mother, or at least a care giver, regurgitated meat for a small one. So, that was how moms without breasts did it.

The conversation ended as the four groups turned in among themselves.

"They're interested in what we have to offer them," Jacques whispered softly to Kris. "Now they're wondering what they can us to give to get this stuff for them. Notice that our Ostrich is heading over to stand with his pa. This may get interesting."

If it got interesting, it did at a very low decibel level. There were a lot of backward glances at Kris and her Marines. No doubt, the difference between the trade rifles and the M-6's was not lost on the local elders and hunters.

Finally, the shipyard Ostrich came back to Kris. "They want to talk more among themselves. I have told them that you want land within our hunting grounds to grow your food. Lots of seeds for you to eat. We do not grow seeds. We gather some to eat with our meat, but this is a very strange thing for us," he said, dipping his head up and down on his long neck.

"I see. I see your ways. I have eaten in your mess. I see how one can work here and eat food from somewhere else. Still, it took me many days to grasp such a strange hunt. I will try to help my egg warmer see your strange hunt, but it may take more than one sunset."

"Let us eat what our hunters have brought from far away and gnaw at this," Kris said.

"Yes, this is a lot to gnaw on among many wise elders," the young leader said.

Kris settled back in her gun truck, out of the sun that was growing hotter. One Marine gun rig brought back a load of meat with some very enthusiastic hunters. In no time at all, it was headed back with a new collection of hunters as those from the first hunt joined the talk with their elders.

Through the morning, trucks came back and left just as quickly.

"Are they hunting out this area?" Kris asked Jacques.

"Each shift is going someplace else," he told Kris. "I think that is what is so exciting to these hunters. One hunts near the rocks. Another hunts close to the trees. Still another near the watering hole. They're excited to see how many places they can hunt in one day. I think the gun rigs are just as exciting as the rifles."

"You may have a point," Jack said. He'd been quiet most of the day.

"You okay?" Kris asked.

"I'm on pain meds. Rule one, don't make a fool of yourself," Jack said wryly

"Get off your feet and into the truck," Kris said in not quite an order voice.

Jack didn't argue with her, but with a quick nod to Gunny, did as he was told.

Nelly, how bad was that 'flesh wound'?

Jack's medical records are sealed. I can break in, but I think that would be dishonorable, Kris.

Kris scowled, and settled in to wait. She'd started the ball rolling. There was nothing to do while it rolled around.

As the light gun rigs brought back more food, the discussions among the birds got more animated. Kris had seen enough.

"Nelly, get me Admiral Benson."

"You rang, Admiral," came only a second later.

"Who came up with the idea of designing rifles specifically for the Ostriches?"

"Several, including the boys that were up here working for us. Some folks took them out to a gaming gallery and they loved to shoot, but hated human rifles. They made up one for the shooter game. We modified the design last night and knocked out ten of them. They going over as well as I'd bet?"

"Probably better. How many more have you got?"

"Last time I checked, we had forty done out of one hundred ordered. Why?"

"I need as many as you can get on a longboat, along with eight electric wagons, with say, a single axle trailer for each, and at least four recharging stations."

"Gifts?"

"Gifts to get the idea across that you want to give us gifts."

"They should be down in six hours."

"Nelly, get the transport headed back to the mine. Benson, we'll need as much as this again for the next negotiations."

"I figured as much. I'll have them ready tomorrow morning. Should I drop you down some place to stay tonight?"

"Temporary quarters would be nice."

"I'll get you some prefabs on the drop. Maybe even a few extra gun trucks and trailers."

"Yeah. It looks like this is going to take a while."

"Pipra was wondering if you had a deal inked yet."

"Tell her to hold her horses. Rome wasn't built in a day and I doubt they talk my ancestors out of New York with a few beads and trinkets in one afternoon."

"You touchy?"

"No, I just don't want to go down in the history books with the wrong company."

"Change is heading at these folks with the power of an alien base ship."

"I know, Admiral. I know," Kris said with a sigh.

Talk went on as noon came and went. More food arrived. The hunters were delighted with the rifles. A few of the senior hunters tried to lay claim to the rifles the workers had brought home. Elders may not have known how to read Kris's face, but the way the Marines held their rifles at the ready got attention.

The young workers were not hassled further.

The second pulse of Marines, this time accompanied by electric wagons and more rifles, arrived six hours later before matters got out of hand. One of the hunting parties laid out an airstrip closer to the villages.

Kris distributed the electric carts and wagons, recharging stations and forty rifles with twenty rounds of ammunition among the elders of the four tribes.

That took a lot of pressure off the behavior of many of the young bucks. Now, it was the elders passing out the gifts to their choice people. There was trouble enough there, but those who lost out in that round of gift giving were quick to listen to the workers and present themselves to Jacques for recruitment.

"You give them work. They give you food and rifles," was easily understood.

"I hope these rifles don't start a whole lot of trouble," Jack was heard to mumble.

"No doubt it will," Kris said. "We're surfing the curl of a tidal wave. You got to be quick, careful, and ready to change."

A small camp quickly grew up on the upstream side of the village. Ostriches were amazed when a small box blew up into a large hut, then turned solid as rock when what looked like strange smelling water was sprayed on it. The shower and toilet fascinated them, but their proper use eluded them, even when the young returnees tried to explain it.

Privacy was another thing new to them. Only the words of those who'd been with the humans got across the idea that when a door was closed, you didn't open it and walk in.

Marines standing guard helped.

Kris cuddled up next to Jack and prepared to sleep the night away.

Unfortunately, it didn't work out that way.

3

While the Ostriches fought for honor and fame, they had never had much of anything to fight over. Still, every male had the right to challenge anyone to a fight, anytime. The fights went up to and included kicking their heads off if one didn't run first.

Someone challenged one of the rifle holders to a fight. The first challenge was to one of the hunters who had been given a rifle by his chief. That started it.

Fortunately for the shipyard workers, they put two and two together quickly, and beat feet for the Marine camp. The Marines made it immanently clear that they frowned upon people issuing challenges to those under their protection.

Still, Gunny got Kris up to take in what was happening in the villages located downhill from them, closer to the river.

"It's a bloody mess," he observed.

"I didn't see that coming," Jacques admitted.

"Isn't this why they call economics the dismal science?" Kris said. "When there's too little of what people want, the price goes up. In this case, if you can take it, it's yours. Jacques, would you feel safe bringing me the elders?"

"So long as I don't have a gun and the Marines are in full battle rattle," the anthropologist answered.

Kris looked around her encampment. Most of it was very high tech. "Gunny, get me a fire going." Kris had seen no fire in the Ostrich villages. Something lower tech might be more impressive than indoor plumbing.

Ten minutes later, Jacques and his Marines returned with four very separate and cautious groups of hunters and elders.

"How'd it go?" Kris asked.

"One dumb bird tried to butt chests with a Marine in full battle armor," Jacques said with a rather grim grin. "He'll be a long time butting anyone else."

The groups of elders held back in the shadows beyond the fire.

"Gunny, toss some more cow dung on the fire," Kris ordered. They'd found no wood to burn close to the camp. They had found a lot of the droppings of the grazing animals. The survival manual said it might burn. It did, very brightly.

No surprise, fire appeared to be totally new to the locals. The gathered elders eyed and its light, then the worker Ostriches that stood with the Marines around it. Slowly, they worked their way into the flames light and warmth. They approached, but stayed well away from Kris and her armed and armored Marines, as well as each other.

Kris and baby had had enough squatting; a Marine brought her a chair. She also no longer wanted these birds to think of her as their equal. Her attitude was changing. Theirs needed to change as well.

Kris's eyes swept the birds huddled at the edge of the

fire's light. "I gave you gifts. What have you done with them?" As Kris spoke, Nelly translated.

No one ventured to answer her question.

"Does your tribe use my gifts to feed you or kick heads until you will not have enough hunters to feed you?"

Again, there was no answer from the shame-faced elders.

"Should I take back my gifts?" Kris asked.

The silence to that was broken when one hunter with a rifle muttered something.

HE SAID NO ONE WILL TAKE BACK HIS ROCK THROWER.

"Gunny, put a round between his legs."

"Corporal,"

In a blink, an M-6 came up. A shot rang out and a gout of dust rose between the bird's legs. He jumped up, stung by the dirt and maybe a stone.

He brought his rifle up. He brought it up but he didn't put his finger on the trigger. He did not fire.

Instead, he whirled and ran into the dark.

Kris turned to the senior yard worker. "Have you explained to your people how the rifles need ammunition? No ammunition. No game. It's just a big club."

"I have tried to show them that. Some people have a hard time seeing what they do not want to see."

"Gunny, what kind of ammunition did we distribute?"

"Four stripper clips of five with each rifle. Most of them shot more than that today. It takes them a while to get the hang of a sight picture, ma'am."

"No doubt."

Kris turned back to the elders.

"Can you hold the water in your hands and walk from the river to here?"

That got heads slowly shaking.

"Can you hold the prey herds in one place for you to eat forever?"

More head were shaking.

"I give. You give. I give rifles. I want you to give me land my people can build huts like these on," Kris said, indicating the building behind her. "My people will cause the land to give up food just as my rifles cause the herds to give up meat. We will follow herds that will stay on our land and give us more meat than your herds give you. That is our way. Come and see, and it can become your way."

"Do you want all our land?" one Elder said, standing up, and making a kick with his right leg, no doubt issuing a formal challenge to Kris, if that was her intent.

"We want only parts of your land that you seldom use," Kris said. "You use this land to walk through from one of your hunting grounds to another. We will leave land open for you to walk on, but other land, we will use for our food. As a few hunters have feed many people today, so a hand of our hunters can feed a tribe of our people."

"A hand feed a tribe?" went like a murmur through the elders.

"After the next season of rain, you will see," Kris said.

"My eggborn never went hungry while he was above the sky where you walk," one elder said. Apparently, he was the mighty one. The senior yard worker was standing beside him.

"We do not know hunger," Kris said. At present, it wasn't too much of a lie.

A shot came out of the night, slammed into Kris and knocked her and her chair over.

Kris found herself staring up at the night sky. On the

roof of the hut, a Marine sniper had his rifle up. Three shots answered the one.

"Got him, Gunny," the Marine reported.

Gunny snapped an order and four Marines ran into the night. A minute or so later, they returned dragging the bird who'd muttered before Kris and gotten a round between his legs for his effort.

The Marines deposited the body by the fire. Gunny was just helping Kris up when one Marine offered her the man's rifle.

Kris took it, stripped the bolt, palmed the firing pin, and sniffed the recently fired barrel. She offered the barrel to the shipyard worker.

He sniffed it. "This was just shot. This is the rifle that shot my leader and employer."

Leader was a familiar word on his beak. Employer came out in mangled standard.

"Does anyone doubt this man owes a blood price?" the space station worker demanded of those still squatting in the dirt on the other side of the campfire from Kris.

"But where is her blood?" one asked. Even in the local tongue, Kris could hear the shock.

"You do not beat chest with us," Kris said. "You do not use our own rifles against us," Kris said, taking the rifle bullet from her chest and tossed it to the young worker.

He took the spent round and walked it around the fire for all the elders to get a good look at.

"You have seen what a bullet looks like," the worker said. "If you have bitten into meat and found the bullet that killed it, you have seen a bullet like this. This is such a bullet. Look upon the leader of the star walkers. See that this bullet did no harm to her."

"I think they just realized who they're bargaining with," Jacques whispered to Kris.

"If you sup with the devil, you'll need a long spoon," she said.

"And I don't think they have anything nearly long enough for a handle. You will note, however, that none of them are bowing down to you. I still can't figure out what they use for a god, but you are not one."

"I have no problem with that," Kris said.

"Is there anyone who demands a blood price from me?" Kris said firmly to the gathered elders.

They looked at each other. Finally, the father of the senior yard worker spoke. "His blood was upon his own head. It is you who may demand a blood price."

"I ask no blood price of a fool. Let his blood price be the lesson you learn here. Elders, control your hunters. Let there be no more blood lost over my gifts. Do this, or there will be no more bullets from me when you have used up those I gave you.

"As for this rifle," Kris said, raising the rifle up that had been used to shoot her, she slammed it down. The long wooden stock gave and the rifle was suddenly in two halves.

"That will happen to any gift used against its giver."

The elders now walked into the darkness. The five young birds who had been so excited to return home stayed close to the fire. Jacques went aside with them, then brought them back to nest down close by the fire before returning to Kris.

"None of them ever expected to say it, but they feel safer among us than they do among their own people."

"That won't last. Once they get over the shock of the introduction of rifles, things will settle down."

"And then they'll change some more, Kris. We are a

warm wind blowing through here, stirring up all kinds of new. Some is shiny. Some is just new. I know there's no way to avoid it, but it's still tough to change."

"We'll come up with a better idea of how to manage the next bunch of tribes," Kris said.

"Why not give me the impossible task and call it quits?" Jacques shot back.

Jack was standing in the doorway. "You've got to quit doing this, love."

"Well, at least I had my silks on," was Kris's answer to both of them.

"Ah, ma'am," said the Marine on the roof. "I'm sorry I didn't get him before he shot you."

"If you'd shot him before he took his pot shot, I'd be very upset with you," Kris answered.

"Not nearly as upset as I'm going to be," Gunny muttered from beside Kris.

"Gunny, the Marines are your charge, but keep this in mind. I can't have dead locals showing up without good cause."

"But I can't have dead admirals on my soul, ma'am."

Jack cleared his throat, diplomatically. "Gunny, that's why officers get paid the big bucks."

"If you say so, General."

"I think he just did," Kris said.

"Ma'am," had that sharp twist that said this Gunny did not like what his officers were doing, but they were officers, so he'd put up with them.

So Kris found herself back in Jack's arms, her back cuddled up to his front, and his good hand softly warming baby.

They were not disturbed again that night.

4

Abby was there as Kris awoke. Cool milk and ginger cookies, if not fresh, were still settling to Kris's tummy. Breakfast was field rations, eggs and bacon cooked in ten person meals rather than a combat ready breakfast out of a box.

The senior yard worker was already up and gone into the tribal camps. He returned as Kris finished the part of her breakfast she could stomach. His father and a dozen elders followed.

"My eggborn has showed me the path your rifles follow. If they are not fed, they do not hunt."

"That is the way of it," Kris said.

"What do you want so that I and my followers can feed our rifles?"

"I wish to use some of your land. For that, each full moon, I will give you four of my hands of bullets for each rifle." Alwa's single moon took twenty-four days to circle and did fourteen in a year.

"You broke one of the rifles."

"One of you shot at me. Do not make me break more rifles," was as bare as it was cold.

The elder ducked his long neck. "We must have no more rifles broken," he muttered softly.

Behind him, the other elders ducked their heads.

Then he went on. "What land do you wish to walk?"

"Come with me and we will mark it."

Kris had eight Marine rigs now. She put two or three senior birds in each one of them and drove back to the breaks. She intentionally drove by the transport planes.

"That swallows them up and then they fly higher than any bird," the youngster said.

The elders in Kris's rig held their necks long, tall, and rigid as they eyed it.

"Have you seen it?" the father asked the son.

"It carried me back to you. It was a moon walk to get to the human camp. It was less than a morning to come back."

Now heads did duck low.

Kris marked out the land that she and Jacques had identified on the map. There would be three large blocks of human cultivation, with two large pathways between them and plenty of room to go around them. The Ostriches would have no trouble going from the river in the dry time, to the highlands in the wet time, when the river flooded.

Kris drove from one end of the range to the other, leaving large metal markers with green flags that whipped in the wind at the farthest reaches of the human lands. Kris gave the Ostrich elders their first payment as she returned to the airplane. The second Marine detachment would take the elders home while the plane flew Kris to her next meeting.

The elders spotted the other Ostriches lounging around the plane and would have attacked them if they could have gotten out of the rigs fast enough. Kris could not tell the difference between one Ostrich and the other.

Clearly, they had no trouble doing it.

"I will have none of my rifles used to hunt another of your kind. And I include them as your kind."

"We have hunted them from before the sun rose the first time, and they have hunted us," the senior elder said.

"You did that before the rifles," Kris said firmly. "Do you want the rifles or do you want to hunt them? You choose the path to walk."

The yard worker stepped forward. "My egg warmer, I have run with these people among the sky walkers' hunting parties. They hunt good and we hunt good. The sky walkers are happy with my hunting and their hunting. If you make them choose between us and them, they will choose those who run along fast with them and do not squawk like hatchlings when the prey is in sight."

The elder's neck jerked in several quick ducks at he turned to glance at his fellow elders. "I will have to talk with many hunters to see if there will be no more hunting of the others," he said.

"Just know this," Kris said. "I will be giving them the same rifles and the same bullets if they give us land to use. Hunting them will not be easy. Know that I will see the hunting and I will not turn away from this foolishness."

"Warmer of my egg," the young worker said, stepping between Kris and his father, "we see hatchlings peck at each other. They even bite each other, but do little harm. Then we grow to kicking high and can chomp hard and bleed each other much. Elders tell us how to walk with others and we walk that way. I have seen with my own eyes how hard these sky walkers can kick. They have rifles that make our rifles no better than a chick throwing its first pebble. You do not want to anger these people."

If Kris was any judge of Ostrich body language, the senior was none too happy to be lectured by the junior.

He turned his long neck away from his son as he said, "I will have to see some of what you have seen with my own eyes, my eggborn."

Kris left the elders to stew in all the new she'd dropped on them. While the second Marine detachment took the elders back to their camp, Kris boarded the transport with the first.

"Let's see how much trouble we can cause across the river," she muttered to Jack.

The five yard workers, their rifles in hand, joined Kris's flight out. To her surprise, they approached the other five, sat next to them, and were soon in deep conversation.

"I wonder what that's all about?" Jack said.

"Birds," Admiral Furzah muttered as she took a seat near Kris and Jack. "You can say as much as you want that those things have brains, but all I see is feather brains."

"Please don't eat any of them," Jacques said. "We have enough trouble as it is."

"There's not enough meat on any of them to make a decent meal," the admiral pointed out, and seemed to settle the matter on that point.

Kris's visit to this second collection of tribes went quite different; the conversation among the young Ostriches may have had something to do with it.

As she had before, Kris and her Marines helped the returning workers provide plenty of meat for a feast. They did their hunting under the surprised gaze of the tribes' best hunters.

The young Alwans arranged for Kris's introduction to

the elders. This time, the elders knew that the tribes across the river already had made a deal with the star walkers. In return for land, they had been given the gift of forty rifles and ammunition. With the general outline of a deal already on the table to be passed along to the elders by their young workers, the overall conversation was more about explaining matters than haggling. Jacques made sure that no loose ends were overlooked in the rush by the tribal elders to get their hands on the rifles. They even got around to the electric carts and solar chargers.

Where the tribes on the other side of the river had been so fixated on the rifles, these elders wanted to know more about the carts and what they might do for their own hunters. Kris credited her station workers for helping their elders to look this gift horse over more carefully.

When it was time, Kris provided the rifles. This time, only a few were handed out by the elders to chosen hunters. Most, six or seven per tribe, were awarded as prizes for winning games of strength and skill. That night, Kris got a good night's sleep, uninterrupted by either fights or assassination attempts.

The next morning, the elders traveled with Kris to mark out the land. Some rode in her rigs, others followed in their own electric carts. As her plane lifted off late the next day, it was easy to spot a long stream of small groups of Ostriches already making their way to the guano mine, apparently ready to seek work with the people who offered such nice rewards.

Kris arranged for a doctor to see Jack at the mine. He was cleared for a shuttle flight and Kris was ready to lift out, but the mining supervisor presented her with a minor request.

"Sampson and Mugeridge are still not eating. We rouse

them out of bed and march them off to the digs, but they refuse to work. They just sit there, demanding to talk to you."

"And you'd like me to talk to them."

"No, ma'am, I just wanted you to know what's happening," the former ship skipper said, his lips tight and grim. "I am kind of worried that they'll die on us, Admiral. I just felt like you might want a heads up beforehand. My job here is to dig bird shit, not be an executioner."

Kris just shook her head. "Thanks, Commander, for the heads up. If they're going to do this, be it upon their heads. You can tell them for me that I don't care what they do. They can work and eat or they can sit on a pile of shit and die. Their choice. But whatever they do, they are going to do it here. No place else."

"I'll pass that along," the ex-skipper said.

Kris was back up to the *Wasp*, had gotten in a long bath with Jack and was halfway through a nice dinner in the wardroom before a long line of people caught up with her sharing business pies she just had to get her fingers into.

KRIS LONGKNIFE'S
BAD DAY

Initially, this was the first chapter of Kris Longknife Emissary. However, few people find the government budget process as fascinating as I do. This story bring you up to date on Wardhaven Navy doctrine and policies. If you like that kind of stuff, you'll love this book. If you don't, it's a great bridge between the Kris Longknife of Bold who demands a desk job and the Kris Longknife in Emissary who is only too happy to accept a new job.

A dmiral, Her Royal Highness Kris Longknife, returned from a pleasant lunch with her husband sporting a smile on her face. Five years ago, to this very day she'd demanded a desk job where she could have lunch every noon with Lieutenant General Jack Montoya, RUSMC, and go home to her kids at 1700 every afternoon.

For a while, Kris had kept count of every day she and Jack met for lunch, but somewhere about the end of the first year, she gave that up. Jack was a Marine general and had inspections and field operations that occasionally left her eating a lone lunch at her desk. Kris was type commander for the Battlecruiser Force and had her own inspections to attend, as well as fleet exercises to observe and write up. Sometimes, Jack ended up eating lunch on his own as well.

That reflection cost Kris her smile. Fleet problems always meant her crossing swords with the Battle Fleet and Scout Force type commanders as she defended her battlecruisers from their misuse. Also, during the planning for every fleet problem she'd have to spend way too much time trying to free her battlecruisers from the straightjacket of the exercise's orders so they could go raise hell with battleships and cruisers alike.

After three years of butting her head against the brick wall of the hide-bound Navy bureaucracy, Kris's manual for the proper doctrine for battlecruisers use remained in draft form despite everything she had done to get them signed off.

Kris shrugged, something she'd been doing a lot of lately, and tried to regain her cheerful self. *Five years! Wow.*

The pool on when she'd leave hadn't taken so much as a dollar bet in the last year. They were learning that when this damn Longknife said she was quite tired of being run ragged as a fire chaser for King Raymond I, Grampa Ray to her, she meant it.

Kris opened the door to her outer office. She'd managed to get it repainted in a soft green. The carpet now was a light blue. Neither color was one she could get away with at Nuu house, not with Ruth and John Junior's grubby hands and muddy feet tracking dirt everywhere.

Those were happy thoughts.

But the look on Lieutenant Megan Longknife, Kris's once again *aide de camp,* brought Kris to a halt with a frown slowly overtaking her own face.

"What is it now?" Kris demanded.

The young lieutenant took only a moment to answer, "The draft budget is out." She held up three readers, colored blood red for top secret.

Kris scowled. "Three readers? Is the damn budget so big that one reader can't hold it all?"

"No, Admiral," Megan answered with the firm voice that an adult might take with a petulant three-year-old, "but last year you busted your copy when you tossed it across the room. That cost us a whole day for putting together our rebuttals while I got you another copy. This year I put in for six copies and got three. Please don't break more than two," she said with only a slightly hopeful look for her admiral.

Kris chose to ignore the drama; she wasn't that bad, really. Usually. "So, how bad is it?" Kris growled, advancing on her *aide de camp's* desk like an army with banners.

"I wouldn't know, ma'am. These copies are coded to your thumb," was spoken too innocently for a Longknife, even a Longknife from the side of the family that had fled a quarter of the way across the galaxy to Santa Maria.

"Then why did you ask for six copies and settle for

three?" Kris said, taking the top one of the three offered readers.

"Well, there is talk in the lady's head and rumors around the halls, if you know the right water coolers to drink at," Megan said with the tiniest hint of a conspiratorial shrug, which like most any expression, looked good on the lovely young officer. Kris wondered, as she had so many times, if she was looking at an exact reproduction of herself a few years ago, and swallowed a chuckle that the budget, no doubt, did not deserve.

It was good to have Megan back as her flag lieutenant and aide. She'd been sorry to lose her to ship duty, but the gal's career needed the space tour. Still, Kris had been overjoyed when the young lieutenant put in for the desk guarding Kris's office.

Her last flag lieutenant had been too much in awe of a damn Longknife. Indeed, he was too much in awe of having a job in the Main Navy building and all the stars and birds that hurried down the halls in self-important haste.

With any luck, he was enjoying space duty and had many tales to tell of his time close to the big, powerful, and self-pretentious.

What he couldn't tell anyone about was the secretive junior officer information network that Meg had taken to like a fish to water. Its existence had gone right over his head.

Kris ran her thumb through the sensor, then looked into the tiny hole on the side of the reader. Only then did the reading surface area transform from red with a large TOP SECRET slashed across it and open up to show a comfortable white reading surface.

The first page announced: DRAFT DEFENSE BUDGET,

WARDHAVEN, TOP SECRET UNTIL RELEASED TO PARLIAMENT.

A flip of the page brought her to the index. No surprises, it had the same budget cost centers as last year.

The print was getting smaller, however. Having spent her quite recent thirtieth birthday decanting John Junior from his uterine replicator into this world, Kris found it hard to believe that her eyes were the problem.

Of course, John Junior was now four. Strange how that happened.

With a little help from her friends, Kris would ignore this issue for a while longer.

"Nelly, could you please project the budget on the wall?"

"Aye, aye, Admiral," Nelly responded. She'd gotten more nautical in her language the longer Kris spent at her desk job.

Nelly had been Kris's computer since her first day of school. Upgraded too many times to count, Nelly was now worth nearly as much as one of Kris's battlecruisers. She'd also taken to telling bad jokes and arguing with Kris. Fortunately, today Nelly appeared to be in a helpful mood.

In a blink, the long wall in Kris's office across from the windows transformed itself. The standard bureaucratic beige wall with its large, stylized oil painting of the Battle of System X vanished. Now the first dozen pages of the budget covered it. While the reader had security to squelch just this kind of projection, once again, Nelly had circumvented the best Wardhaven had in order to give Kris what she asked for.

The Executive Summary was short, but not sweet. The bitter pill in the last paragraph, the total size of the budget, had way too many zeros and commas in it. That drew a whistle from Megan.

"Your father's not going to like the price on this thing," Kris's flag lieutenant commented.

Kris shook her head in agreement. Her father had been the prime minister for about as long as Kris could remember. The brief exception had been an embarrassment to all involved and had resulted in a major battle where Kris and a dozen tiny mosquito boats took out a squadron of six huge battleships that threatened to pound Wardhaven back into the stone age.

Kris still shivered when she thought of all the luck that went into wining that fight . . . and all the lives that had been lost under her command. It had been the first but not the last time she'd had to face her own butcher's bill.

There were advantages to commanding a desk.

"No doubt, the politicians will see that every penny squeaks like a pig as it leaves the public purse," Kris said, then added pensively. "Where to start? Nelly, bring up the Jump Fortresses."

Both Kris and Meg whistled when Nelly made that chapter appear.

"They've doubled their budget again this year," Meg exclaimed. "And they project it doubling again next year and for it to stay that way until the end of the Five Year Plan!"

Kris cringed at the budget drain; she could outfit a full fleet of battlecruisers for that cost, but the Jump Fortresses were her own fault.

"I can't wish I never came up with the idea of laser-armed forts guarding the jumps," Kris muttered, shaking her head.

As commander of distant Alwa station, Kris had combined ideas from several good people and figured out a way to keep a dozen battleship-sized lasers ready to take out anything coming through the jumps into the Alwa system. They'd been faced with an infestation of suicide speedsters. If even one of them got through to Alwa, millions would have died. A strong laser presence at each jump had been critical.

However, those lasers didn't need to be armored, just quick to shoot and deadly accurate.

Here on Wardhaven, the government goal was to guard every jump into the system from invasion by a huge alien raiding base ship and its hundreds of half million ton warships.

Eager to make her father, his government, and the people of Wardhaven feel safer from the blood thirsty alien monsters that Kris had located in her circumnavigation of the galaxy, she had innocently suggested building small space fortresses. Equipped with the new 24-inch lasers and stationed some 200,000 kilometers from the jump, they'd need small engines to move them if the jump moved. They shouldn't have cost more than two battleships.

Or eight battlecruisers, as the Battle Force people were very quick to point out.

Two years ago, work had started on five fortresses to guard each of the five jumps into the Wardhaven system. The last of the jump forts should have been finished this year.

Then, an overeducated idiot jumped to the conclusion that if one fortress was good, two fortresses would be twice as good for the protection of the electorate. Last year, the budget had doubled to provide for ten forts. The cost of constructing the forts should have come down this year and finished up the next.

There was a picture of the first completed fortress on the screen. It was as big around as the space stations Kris had used on Alwa station, a two kilometer in diameter can with thirty 24-inch lasers always pointed at the jump.

So, what had happened to jack up the cost and send it smashing through the out-year budget?

"Oh, good grief," Megan said, and pointed her wrist unit at one place on the wall. Nelly quickly highlighted it.

"They're expanding the forts to hold bigger lasers and adding a third fortress at each jump with beam guns!" Megan exclaimed.

Kris let out a long sigh. Why hadn't she thought of that?

She was the only battle commander with actual experience with the monstrous beam guns. Three beam ships, weighing in at a half million tons or more, and with reactors that could easily power half a planet, had helped her defeat four alien hoards by chipping tiny but unbelievably heavy darts off of a neutron star.

The beam ships themselves had been brand new, untried, and cranky. During the battle, one almost blew itself up and a second had to limp home with half of it reduced to junk. All this without taking a single hit from the alien monsters who wanted all of humanity, and any other living thing in the galaxy, dead.

Still, the idea of stationing beam guns on Jump Fortresses to punch huge holes in incoming alien base ships and the battering rams they'd developed to force jumps was a neat idea, assuming whoever was behind this new budget drain had refined the equipment and were ready to operate it at a wartime tempo.

"They'll need a huge fort," Kris half muttered to herself, "and they'll need to be close enough to the jump to spot ships coming through." Kris had stationed her three beam ships around a dead planet a third of an astronomical unit from the neutron star, some 50,000,000 kilometers. It had still taken the beam almost three minutes to cover that distance, even at the speed of light.

In Kris's battle, the neutron star had stayed an unmoving target. A lot could happen, however, in the six minutes or so that it took a beam ship to spot an invasion force, lock in a target, and get a beam back at it from that far away. "I wouldn't recommend that they hold the beam stations as far back as I had my beam ships from the neutron star," Kris mused.

"There is a long discussion of that in the supporting material, Kris," Nelly said, and the screen changed from pages one though six of the long budget document to pages 637 through 642. Nelly highlighted two full pages.

Thank heavens for Nelly, Kris thought as she studied the supporting documents. There had been tests, a lot of tests. The 24-inch lasers for the forts had initially been identical to those on battleships and battlecruisers. Somebody had taken that idea and run with it. After all, different guns meant a different development cycle and construction base.

All of that sucked up more money for design staff and fabrication plants, of course.

Since the laser developers had huge forts to work with, they'd doubled the length of the lasers, added extra reactors and jacked up the power in the laser and its duration.

All that heat had to go somewhere, so the outer hull of the forts was honeycombed with heat sinks for cooling. At least when the battle started, the forts would have huge cooling sails. No doubt, those would be blown away quickly, but if the forts snapped up the incoming alien warships fast enough, the sails might survive until well into the fight.

Megan whistled, and so did Kris. "They tested those jacked up lasers against thirty meters of basalt backed up with twenty meters of ice," Kris whispered.

The last time she'd fought the aliens, they'd taken to coating their ships with stone, usually granite. Meters of it. That hadn't stopped Kris's battlecruisers from blowing them away by aiming two, three or even four lasers for the same place on the target. These new lasers would punch through more armor than those ships had carried and still have enough power left over to slash through ship's structure, equipment, and crew.

Kris frowned. "How are we going to force a jump defended like that?" she murmured, half to herself.

Meg raised both eyebrows. "It kind of looks like the defense has taken a huge jump over the offense. Do you think this will make war impossible between humans?"

Kris ran a worried hand through her hair. She'd let it grow longer; it made for some new fun with Jack. She shook her head against that rabbit hole and dodged away from going down it mentally.

"The ultimate weapon has never stopped humans from trying to kill each other. No doubt we and Battle Fleet will soon be tasked to come up with a way to force a jump defended by our own forts."

Kris dumped that into a pigeon hole to mull over in her spare time, of which she now occasionally had some, and read the test of concept for the beam fortresses.

The beam fortresses would be four kilometers across and ten klicks long. They'd chosen to station them about a million kilometers back from each jump. That would give them a bit more than three seconds to know the jump had been breached. If you assumed three seconds to process the target, and another three for the laser beam to get back and hit something, it totaled out at nine seconds, give or take a few nanoseconds.

In a space battle, a lot could happen in nine horribly long seconds.

Kris stared at the ceiling, seeing the jump into the Alwa system she'd tried to hold, but been forced to fall back from during the First Battle for the Alwa System. The aliens' huge half million ton warships were slow to come through at first. They also kept their distance from each other, like ponderous dancing pachyderms, and Kris's guard force had blown them away, one after another.

However, as more failed to report back on what was on the other side of the jump, the Enlightened Master on the alien base ship had gotten more rambunctious with his massive ships, and in the end, Kris had watched as they tiptoed through the jump at one second intervals.

Tiptoed was the right word. The half million ton alien warships were traveling at only a few kilometers an hour to keep the jump from sending them off to God only knows where in a sour jump.

From dead slow, it took time to accelerate something that massive. Every second it took was time given the fire control systems on Kris's ships to target them and lay a hellish amount of laser fire on them.

A lot of alien ships died before they could get away from the murder hole.

Kris considered one hundred or so alien warships trying to force a jump held by sixty jacked up 24-inch lasers on two forts.

With the alien coming through the jump at one second intervals, and the defensive lasers firing two, maybe three times a minute, each alien warship was likely to take three or four hits within five seconds of cruising through the jump.

Kris shook her head. The aliens would face a murderous

task, getting their forces through a well-guarded jump into human space.

It was also unlikely that they'd have any chance at surprise. Picket buoys now stood vigilant at every jump within ten jumps of Wardhaven. Indeed, all of human space was out-posted against any surprise attack.

Not only would the jump forts be gunning for the alien raiders, but the battleships and battlecruisers would be on alert and stationed close to support the forts, possibly even closer in. When the fortress's guns whacked hard, the battle fleet would be in place to finish it off quickly.

And when the base ship, hulking big as a small moon came through, it would face the beam fortress a good two million klicks back. Say, seven seconds to spot the intruder, three seconds to study its movements, then another seven seconds for the beams to arrive.

Kris shivered. The beam wasn't quite like the device that had been found on Santa Maria. The humans researching it called it the Disappearing Box and were sure that it was a leftover from the Three Alien Races that built the jump points.

Some teenage girls had found the box, opened it, and pointed it at a mountain. They weren't sure exactly what they did next, but somehow, they activated it and the top three thousand meters of a distant mountain had vanished. Just disappeared.

After eighty years of studying the box, human scientists had no idea how or where that mountain top had vanished to. However, in the process of looking for one thing, they'd stumbled upon something else – the beam gun.

Kris had seen the beams focused on a neutron star and used to drive off a fifteen-thousand-ton chip hardly the size of the diamond on the engagement ring Jack kept urging her to let him buy. The tiny chip had smashed ships; Kris had yet to see what happened when the beam was widened and aimed at a structure.

According to the budget support, that test would be completed in, Kris glanced at her calendar, two weeks. So, the budget grenadiers intended to spend a whole hunk of money on a weapon that hadn't even been tested yet. Kris shook her head.

"I'll have to keep my eyes peeled for those results," Kris told herself. There was no reason why she couldn't schedule herself to attend the test. She took a deep breath, let it out, and focused on the screen. "Okay, Nelly, enough dodging, what did the budget gods give us this year and how much will it raise my blood pressure?"

One glance at the Battlecruiser Force line items and Kris's frown went to a full scowl.

She had asked for thirty-two of the new battlecruisers: four squadrons of eight ships each. One for Alwa, two for planetary defense, and one for long range patrols to spot alien raider incursions before they got too close to human space.

"We only got twenty-four ships, Kris," Megan said.

Kris shook her head as she considered that development, then said, "We'll have to short someplace or go to six ship squadrons. There are days when I really regret that I can't blow something up."

Meg gave her boss an encouraging look, and Kris tried to make herself be reasonable.

"The new 24-inch lasers are big," her aid pointed out.

To handle twenty of them properly, the new design came in at 75,000 tons, a fifty percent jump in displacement. To stay inside the 50,000 ton size of the 22-inch ship, she would have had to cut the number of guns from twenty to twelve. A compromise design of 65,000 tons could properly support sixteen. Kris had gone with the bigger ship; she hoped her decision wouldn't cost more than she was prepared to pay.

"There's money in the budget for upgrading twenty-four of the most recently constructed battlecruisers. It will replace the old 22-inch lasers with the new 24-inch ones," Megan said, doing her best to sound encouraging.

Kris nodded. Such an upgrade would have been impossible without the Smart Metal^{TM}. With it, the yards could open the ship up like a fileted fish, remove the old lasers, insert the new ones, add in an extra fusion reactor for more power, and zip her back up. Of course, you didn't get a new battlecruiser for this; and you also had to add in another 15,000 tons of Smart Metal^{TM}. Even then, you still could only support sixteen of the new guns. It did, however, give Kris another two dozen ships that could reach out and touch some alien raiders at 270,000 klicks.

Last time Kris had fought the aliens, their newest lasers had just been starting to demonstrate a range of 140,000 klicks. Except for some probing around Alwa, a human outpost all the way on the other side of the galaxy, the aliens that wanted all life in the galaxy dead, except for themselves, had not been heard from in the last five years.

Kris regularly found herself, late at night, wondering what the monsters who looked too damn much like us, were up to.

"Okay, okay," Kris said, knowing she was wasting time. Her beloved battlecruisers had come up short in the budget battle. How bad was it for the Battle Force and Scout Force?

Before the battlecruisers, those two had been all of the space-going Navy there was. Battle Force designed, built, and developed doctrine for the battleships of the fleet. Scout Force did the same for the cruisers and destroyers who did the scouting and escorting of merchant ships when that became necessary.

In Kris's opinion, the battlecruisers with big lasers eliminated the need for battleships, and their fast speed drastically reduced the need for a scouting force. Kris had defended the Alwa system with a fleet of battlecruisers and a small number of auxiliaries. She didn't see a need for expensive battleships or weak cruisers.

Unfortunately, Kris didn't get to make the call for the entire fleet.

Nelly flipped the screen to show the section that covered the Battle Force. Megan's young eyes spotted what Kris was looking for, flinched, and made a grab for the red reader.

Kris spotted the main line items and let out a definitely un-princess-like series of explicatives. She would have hurled the reader at the wall, but Megan had her hands on it. For a moment, two Longknifes wrestled for its possession.

"You promised me I could throw two against the wall," Kris growled.

"But we've got two whole weeks of working with it, Admiral. If you bust this one, you'll only have one backup left."

"But it would feel *so* good," Kris grouched.

The younger Longknife just shook her head. The junior officer had no respect for authority. At least not the authority of her distant cousin, Her Royal Highness Admiral Kris Longknife.

But then, Kris had come to recognize that she needed someone at her elbow who was loyal and wouldn't let her walk all over her. Someone besides the budget masters.

"Okay, Lieutenant, you hold on to the reader and keep it out of harm's way. Nelly, enlarge that section on battleships. I want to read it from my desk," Kris said. As she paced towards it, she took off her uniform coat, hung it on a coat rack, sat, and put her feet up on her desk.

"Now, let's see how bad it is."

Kris didn't have to study the writing on the wall for very long before she was shaking her head. "They did it again. *He* did it again."

"Twelve more battleships," Megan said.

"Yes, another twelve dinosaurs. Overweight and oversized targets that cost four times what a battlecruiser does and needs four times the crew to fight it," Kris spit out.

Kris's battlecruisers carried twenty lasers, all firing forward or aft, with fifteen degrees of wiggle room to aim them. These twelve new battleships would carry twenty-four of the new 24-inch lasers mounted three to a turret, four forward, four aft. The turrets allowed the lasers to fire through 150 degrees away from the long axis of the ships: up or down, fore or aft.

Battleships had been designed that way ever since humans had been building those over-armed and armored behemoths for war.

The problem with this kind of design was the vast amount of open space that it required inside the armored hull of the ship. The long lasers had to swing through a complete circle inside the ship as it trained on a target. The 24-inch lasers were the longest yet. The new battleships were 150,000 tons; half again larger than the monstrous 100,000 ton battleships Kris had when she fought to save Wardhaven.

That these battleships took up twice the tonnage of a battlecruiser for only four more big lasers was bad enough. However, all those voids inside the ship for the guns' movement meant the hulls were huge. All of that oversized hull now had to be covered with crystal armor.

Even worse, some battleship admiral had gotten it in his head that if the battlecruisers had crystal ten centimeters thick, the battleships should have twenty centimeters of the stuff!

Kris had a strong hunch that this was not only a costly requirement, but likely a very bad idea. While the crystal did a great job of absorbing a laser hit, distributing the energy throughout all the crystal cladding and radiating it back out into space, there was still heat involved. Lots of it.

The Earth battlecruisers that had brought the first crystal out to Alwa had not fared well when they first went into battle. The crystal heated up when hit, that heat was transferred to the hull with what had been serious consequences.

Alwa Station battlecruisers were quickly clad with crystal, but the Smart Metal™ behind the cladding was honeycombed with voids filled with reaction mass circulating through it, carrying off the heat and keeping the hull from melting.

Kris wanted to test the twenty-centimeter armor in a live fire shoot. She suspected that the middle of the armor would heat up to destructive levels. She had the scientific calculations to back her up.

Unfortunately, the battleship admirals had their own calculations that said there was no problem. It didn't come as a surprise to Kris that those calculations were on Nuu Enterprises' stationary.

Her Grampa Al was at it again.

Kris's Grampa Al ran a significant portion of Wardhaven's manufacturing economy. Kris was a major shareholder in Nuu Enterprises and had never been able to spend half of her annual dividends. To spend even that much had taken funding a bank on a distant planet that jump-started its entire economy.

Nuu Enterprises was huge. Last year, Grampa Al's spaceship building yards had won the contracts for eight of the battleships in the budget. An old crony of his had gotten the other four.

For the last three years, all the battlecruisers had been built in yards not a part of Nuu Enterprises. Grampa Al was not happy about that. Kris, however, had been untouched by any charges centering around a conflict of interest.

With a heavy sigh, Kris eyed the battleship construction program. She understood the battleship admirals. They'd spent their entire careers in those huge unwieldy ships, but they were able to be educated. At least some of them were. However, with Grampa Al pushing hard for more battleships and spreading the work out to subcontractors all over Wardhaven, it was turning into an impossible job to zero the battleship account and use that money to plus up the battlecruisers.

For five years, Kris had struggled to persuade Navy, Parliament, and the general public, that battlecruisers were the best solution to their defense needs. For five years, the conservative elements in the Navy, Parliament, and people, had given her some of what she needed while still permitting the other cost centers to grow as the fear of the alien raiders became palpable.

Of course, Kris had done her best to grow that fear by standing in front of any civic group that would give her a podium to talk from. Her spiel was simple. The aliens were out there and they would sterilize any human planet if they were given the chance. Humanity needed to make sure they didn't allow them that chance.

Being a princess helped when you had an agenda to push on people.

Unfortunately, admirals, politicians, and men of business had their own agenda, and could push back as much, if not more, than a princess. When their careers or jobs were on the line, they could push back very well, thank you.

Kris glanced through the rest of the battleship building plan. The twenty-four battleships from the last two years' construction plans were made of Smart Metal^{TM}, would be increased to 150,000 tons, and get the 24-inch lasers. Battleships before then had been made of conventional materials and could not be modified.

There were strong hints in the budget narrative that the entire battle fleet would need to be replaced, and replaced not according to the established Forty Year Recapitalization Plan, but much, much, faster.

That wouldn't bother Kris at all . . . if they just replaced them with cheaper battlecruisers that required far less crew.

"You done, Admiral?" Megan asked.

Kris shook her head. She felt very much like she'd been run over by a truck . . . for the fifth time. "Megan, do you see any reason that we can't just reuse the same rebuttal that we presented last year?"

"No, ma'am."

"Is the Scout Force just as bad?"

Nelly flipped to the summary of the cruiser, destroyer, and smaller escort section. It left Kris shaking her head more.

These ships were just too small to stand in any defensive line against half-million ton alien warships with hundreds upon hundreds of lasers. True, the alien lasers were short ranged, but if they got within range of you, you died. The lasers on the cruisers had less range than the alien lasers.

Grand Duchess Vicky Peterwald had warned Kris of the disaster that befell her late, unlamented stepmother's forces when the destroyers under her command had been ordered to make a classical run in a missile attack.

The longer range of the new guns created far too large a killing space for the destroyers to survive long enough to get within missile range. Those destroyers that launched from a safe distance managed to escape. Their missiles, however, had been blotted out well before they could do any damage.

No, the battlecruisers were just as fast and nimble as the cruisers and destroyers, jinking about fast enough to mess with any alien fire control solution and hitting back with battleship-sized lasers.

Yes, different classes of ships had served a purpose seventy or even seven years ago.

Now, however, with battlecruisers available, different classes of ships were no longer needed. The battlecruisers could slug it out in a battle line, while speeding around as fast as any destroyer. It was time to change, and change was cheaper than the old way.

Why didn't everyone else see what was so clear to Kris?

She had drawn up a new manual on battle doctrine that made the optimum use of the battlecruiser's speed, maneuverability, and offensive weapons systems. It was still circulating for comments three years after she finished it. She'd sent it out and gotten a ton of comments. She'd responded to some comments with changes to the draft manual. She'd answered others with clear and cogent arguments. That done, she'd sent the revised version out for comments again.

She'd been through six comment cycles and was no closer to getting her manual finalized.

Her new doctrine had been tested in fleet exercises . . . by ships not under her command and officers that didn't appear to have read her manual. What they didn't botch, the umpires ruled a failure.

Being a damn Longknife with combat experience did not mean a damn thing where the entrenched bureaucrats were concerned.

Kris took her feet off her desk and ran a worried hand through her hair. "Meg, throw together a rebuttal to this year's budget using last year's argument."

"If I can use some of Nelly's spare capacity, I'll have it on your desk first thing tomorrow morning, Admiral."

"Nelly?" Kris asked.

"I'd be happy to work with Lieutenant Longknife, Kris."

"Good," Kris said, then reflected a bit and added. "Oh, Megan, how's the betting pool going about when I'll call it quits and ask for space duty?"

"It's still there, ma'am," Megan said. She knew what would come next; Kris had done this a couple of times over the last three years.

"What do you have to pick now? A week? A month?" Kris asked?

"A month, ma'am."

"Buy a ticket for me and one for you." Nelly popped a calendar up before Kris even asked. This month was half gone. "For next month."

"Yes, ma'am."

"Nelly, order up the car and tell Jack to meet me in the basement."

"It isn't quite five yet, Kris."

"Tell Jack I've had a lousy day."

Only a few seconds later, Nelly reported, "He'll be there before you are."

KRIS LONGKNIFE'S BLOODHOUND

In Kris Longknife Furious, Kris is hauled off to Mushashi to stand trial. With loose ends left behind, she asks a dogged investigator to get to the bottom of something she could not. Follow Senior Chief Agent-in-Charge Foile as he gets a tour of the ugly underbelly of the Longknife legend.

1

Kris Longknife stood alone in the middle of her prison.

So what else was new?

That her prison was an admiral's in port cabin didn't calm the roiling of her emotions. Her mouth was dry and her stomach seemed ready to leap out of her mouth.

She had failed.

Not only had she failed to meet with her Grandfather Al, she'd almost gotten her best friends killed.

Jack killed!

They were just getting to know each other and one of her wild goose chases had damn near gotten Jack and Penny gassed!

What was even a Longknife doing with Sarin gas, much less using it on three stories of his penthouse offices?

Kris wanted to scream.

What she really wanted to do was crawl back into Jack's arms and pretend the world wasn't there.

Better yet, pretend that she hadn't just turned herself

over to Musashi justice. Justice that could end with her kneeling, waiting for the headsman's cut.

The back of her neck itched. She didn't scratch it.

Instead, she took three deep breaths, rolled her shoulders to get some of the tension out, and smiled at this, her pursuer. Her Javier.

Wardhaven Bureau of Investigations Senior Chief Agent in Charge Foile even looked the part. Tall and rail thin, he wore a tan raincoat cinched in at the waist and a brown fedora hat. The hat came off immediately as he entered her borrowed quarters.

The agent had the somewhat dazed look of a civilian who had just been lead through the maze of passageways, ladders and hatches that was a warship. The look vanished as he spotted Kris. His eyes narrowed and Kris find herself facing an appraisal more calculating than she was used to. He paused as their gaze locked.

Kris struggled to keep her face bland if not innocent. She found herself fighting the need to blurt out her entire life story to those hawkish eyes.

She kept her mouth shut and swallowed hard.

The agent stepped forward and gave Kris a slight bow from the neck. "Lieutenant Commander, Her Royal Highness Kristine Longknife, I presume," he said with just a twitch of a smile at the corner of his lips.

His gentle formality gave Kris her opening to fall back into her royal persona. She offered him her hand. "After tonight, I may be back to just Kris. I'm not even sure the Longknife applies."

Foile took the hand. For a moment, Kris thought he'd bend and kiss it. Instead, he shook it.

"Your father had me chasing after you for the last several

days," he said. "I doubt he would do that if he planned to disinherit you."

Kris had to smile at that. The agent was so innocent of the internal workings of the family that spawned her. "Don't be too sure. Water seems to be a lot thicker than blood where my family is concerned. Now," Kris said, and pointed him at an overstuffed chair, "you said you had questions."

Foile settled into the offered chair without breaking eye contact with Kris. Upon reflection, she took one across from him. Unfortunately, that left Jack alone on the couch.

No more cuddles tonight, did not come out in a sigh.

The agent did not let the silence go long. He steepled his fingers, eyed her over them and said, "May I first say that you have led me on quite a chase. No matter where I was, you'd just left. Professionally, I must admire you."

"I had a lot of good help," Kris said with a light chuckle. "Jack here, and Penny. She's asleep in her new quarters. At least I hope she's getting some rest."

The agent canted his head a tiny bit. "And others?" he said evenly.

"No one helped us," Kris said, keeping her words even and her face bland. No doubt the agent would take her answer for a lie, but good people did not deserve to be dragged down into this, her latest fiasco.

Foile raised an eyebrow.

Kris recognized that eyebrow. She'd suffered under it from her Grampa Trouble and, on rare occasions, from her father, the Prime Minister. She's met it from quite a few Navy officers. She'd learned to keep her mouth shut and not even blink.

Today, she folded her hands in her lap and waited patiently for this to pass.

When the silence had stretched, and was in danger of bending, the man gave just a hint of a smile and spoke. "Your father asked me to catch you before you got yourself killed and others with you. I did not catch you, but you seem to have not gotten yourself killed."

Kris breathed a sigh of relief that the eyebrow thing was over and gave Jack a wide-open smile from her heart. "I'm rather well practiced at that."

Agent Foile seemed to settle back into his chair, as if she'd passed some sort of test. Then he went on.

"There is the matter of why you almost got yourself killed this evening. I asked your father about that, and he told me to forget it. He strongly hinted I should forget the entire last week."

Kris shrugged. "I imagine so. Father does tend to want to forget problems he can't solve," she said softly, trying not to let any bitterness slip into her words.

"I'm having a hard time forgetting you risked your life just to talk to your grandfather. And the extent he went to avoid you."

But Kris needed to dodge, not play into some trap this wily agent no doubt was setting. "Sarin gas. That was a bit extreme. Are you sure he gassed the place?"

Agent Foile shrugged. "I told you what I was told. I did not check out the facts, and you did kind of trash the building in your exit."

Kris allowed herself a hearty laugh. From the couch, Jack joined in. It was good to hear him laugh.

"Yes," Kris admitted, "that exit was spectacular, even by my standards. I hope everyone got out of the building. We restored power to the elevators."

"Yes, I know," the agent said. "From what I heard, the place was empty when you left the building."

Kris breathed a sigh of relief at that. But before Kris could enjoy that for a moment, the agent was back at her.

"But what was so important that you risked your life to see your grandfather?"

Kris raised both eyebrows and answered his question with one of her own. "And why was he so intent on not letting me get a word in edgewise?"

To her surprise, the agent's answer was an even, "Exactly."

Kris leaned back in her chair, weighing the options that answer seemed to open up to her. She glanced at Jack; he raised an expressive eyebrow of his own.

She eyed the agent again. "Are you sure you want to know?"

The agent didn't even flinch at the question. His answer was as even as she'd ever heard. "I pursued you for four days. I forced myself on your father, the Prime Minister, and I came all the way up here and managed to crash your present security. By the way, are you seeking political asylum?"

That twist surprised Kris, but she had her answer already prepared for whomever asked it. "I've turned myself in. I expect I'll be facing a Musashi court in a few days."

Maybe she should have left it at that. Maybe the agent had intended to flinch away from the larger question. Maybe she should have kept her mouth shut.

But then, when have I ever?

"But, back to your question. Once again, I must ask you, do you really want to know the answer? If I tell you, you will likely never sleep as soundly as you have."

Agent Foile sat back in his chair. Now his hands grasped its upholstered arms. He seemed to think long and hard. No doubt, if Father had called on him, he was a good and faithful servant of the people of Wardhaven. Did he really want to be initiated into all the twists and turns of the inner circles of those he served?

He took a deep breath and leaned forward. "Can what you tell me what might be any worse than what I'm imagining?"

"Very likely," Jack cut in from his place on the couch. "It's dangerous to get too close to one of these damn Longknifes."

Kris sighed. Jack had a life before he got too close to her. What had she given him in return?

The agent did not flinch. Not even a little bit. "I suspect I have been too close to you Longknifes ever since your father summoned me to his office. Enough beating around this bush. Would you please answer my question?"

Kris could only shake her head and give the man a gentle smile. "Unfortunately, I am not all that sure what the answer is to your question. I assume you know that I seem to have started a war with some hostile aliens on the other side of the galaxy."

"It was in the all the news," Foile said in a matter-of-fact voice that made Kris smile. "My Agent Chu, a fan of yours, made sure I saw the worst of it," he said, sounding like a father who had been dragged off to a rock concert. "Then, suddenly it wasn't there anymore."

"Yes," Kris said, trying not to sound as forlorn as she felt by someone else drawing that conclusion. "There seem to be major differences in high places regarding just how to respond to the hot potato I dropped in their laps. My great-grandfather Ray, King Raymond I, to you, appears to be trying to raise a Navy without raising taxes."

"How's that working for him?" Foile asked.

Kris knew that the question was a throw away. She smiled and answered, "Not so good. Quite a bit of resistance all around. But it's his son, my grandfather Al's reaction, that is causing me trouble."

There, she'd let the cat out of the bag.

The agent canted his head. "What is his reaction?" came at Kris evenly. The pounce might be soft and quiet, but the force of it was overwhelming.

Kris only reflected for a second before laying all her cards face up on the table. "Nothing, officially, but there's chatter, not a lot of it, but it seems that Grampa Al wants to take a different tact from his father. Being the hard-headed business man that he is, it appears he wants to get the aliens talking to him, to establish trade. Whereas the excitable and shoot 'em up types like Ray and me only get them shooting first and neither asking nor answering questions."

The agent took her words in without reaction. He seemed to mull them over for a moment. When he spoke, it was a question.

"What do you think your grandfather Al will try to do?"

Kris took a deep breath. She opened her mouth, but nothing came out. She took another breath, let it out slowly and crept up on her worse nightmare.

"How about sending out a trading fleet loaded with all the goodies that we make?"

Foile pursed his lips in thought, then leaned forward, slipping to the edge of his seat, "And if these bad actors capture the fleet?"

Kris scowled and prepared herself to dive deeper into that nightmare.

Jack got there first. "They get all the computers and navigational material to take them right back to us." he said.

Then he rose from the couch to started pacing out his nervous energy.

Kris envied him his active release, but stayed in her chair, hands now folded tightly in her lap.

"A lot of good people died under my command," she said. "Every ship that was hit, dropped its reactor containment and blew themselves to atoms so that the aliens could get no navigational data from them. It looks like Grampa Al will give it to them on a silver platter."

Now the agent nodded. He seemed to smile into himself. "This was what you wanted to question him about?" he said as if he had finally solved the perfect crime.

"Yes." Kris said, giving the word all the finality it could carry.

"And rather than talk to you, or tell you some lie, he ran away."

"Yes," Kris said, then added with her own raised eyebrow. "Interesting reaction."

"Very interesting," the agent agreed. He seemed to realize he was on the edge of his seat. He forced himself to settle back, but if he was trying to relax, it didn't look like he succeeded.

"You see why I was willing to risk everything to get a few words in," Kris said.

"I do," the agent said, "and may I say that I'm glad that I didn't keep you from getting as far as you got." He chuckled. "I don't often fail. I'm glad I picked this time to have one of my rare breaches."

Kris shrugged and waved limply at the quarters that were her prison. "I did fail. Now all I can hope for is to get my day in court and present my case to the public at large. Clearly, I will not be talking about vague rumors and innuendoes for which I can produce no basis in fact."

The agent nodded vaguely, apparently lost in thought. When he spoke, it was with a smile. "On the other hand, it is frequently my job to produce just the sort of facts you lack."

"Be careful," Kris said. She said that a lot. It usually didn't do much good.

Jack ceased his pacing. "While her Grampa Al might not be willing to use violence against Kris here, his subordinates, or their helpers, people have been known to get very enthusiastic in their effort to get into his good graces. Remember 'will no one rid me of this troublesome priest?' The same could be said of a princess or a cop."

The agent nodded at the warning, but his smile grew wider. "Minor minions are wont to go off half-cocked. However, they are often the ones that crack under pressure and give us our first handle on a rope that leads up the chain of evidence."

The agent paused. Kris could almost see him organizing his thoughts, his plans. They cascading out behind his eyes.

"I think I know a couple of trees to shake," he finally said. "This could be very challenging. Challenging and fun."

"You have a weird sense of fun, then," Jack said.

You're one to talk, said the look Kris shot at him.

So, sue me, he silently shot right back.

The agent stood purposely, then paused, "One word, Princess. If memory serves, Musashi still has capital punishment."

Kris nodded. "Your memory is correct. Nelly advised me of it before we landed on the *Mutsu*, but thank you for the thought."

Kris paused, trying to figure out if there was anything she could do to help this man, this bloodhound who was willing to take on an impossible search for her.

"If I may add, if you insist on taking on this quest for a

damsel . . . and all humanity . . . in distress, you might want to talk with my brother Honovi. He's a member of parliament and not as blind to some things as my father. You might also want to talk to my Grampa Trouble."

The agent laughed. It was something that started deep in his belly and rose to light up his face. "If you mean General Tordon, I talked with him. He was a most reticent witness."

Kris joined in with a chuckle of her own. "He'll loosen up when you get to know him. Tell him I sent you and that I dropped the Grampa Al monkey on your back."

"Thank you," the agent said, then hastened to correct any misperception. "Not for the Grampa Al monkey, but for the secret handshake for General Trouble."

"Just remember," Kris said, shaking her head in warning. "He's trouble for everyone, even me. Oh, another thing. I left my luggage in the Downside elevator station. Is there any chance you could send it on to the *Mutsu*?"

"The police impounded it, but with no case filed, I can likely get it loose."

"Thank you."

"There is just one more matter, Princess. One of my agents, Leslie Chu is a great fan of yours. Is there any chance I might have your autograph?"

"I have a fan club?" Kris said, not believing her ears.

"It seems so," the agent assured her.

Jack just shook his head.

Kris found this almost as hard to accept as an Iteeche Death Ball appearing off her bow. She'd adjusted to that; she could adjust to this. "Is there any paper here?"

"I can print out one of your pictures," Nelly said, and the admiral's desk began spitting out a print. Kris took it from the printer, sat at the desk and found a pen. She thought for a moment, signed it with a flourish, and then added.

"Sorry I missed you."

The agent allowed her another one of his hearty laughs and, with a solemn bow from the waist, turned to take his leave.

2

Late the next morning, Senior Chief Agent in Charge Foile knocked at the front door of Nuu House. The portico and wood carved door was either imposing or intimidating, depending on your perspective.

Agent Foile considered it an interesting piece of history.

From nowhere in particular a voice inquired, "Who may I say is calling?"

"I am Taylor Foile, calling on General Trouble."

He'd considered his words carefully. Intentionally, he'd dropped his official credentials. He was on leave. His boss had signed papers giving him a month off. This was *not* bureau business. And, having been tasked by Kris to meet and seek the help of the legend, it seemed appropriate to use the legend's name.

A long moment later, the door opened and Taylor found himself face to face with the legend himself.

"General Trouble?"

"Agent Foile, I presume."

"Please call me Taylor. I'm on leave for the next month."

The legend raised a questioning eyebrow, but said nothing.

Before the silence stretched, Taylor asked, "May I come in and is there any place we can talk in private?"

"I assume you'd prefer someplace less intimidating than the room we last met in?"

"Please. Your great-granddaughter Kris has asked me to talk with you."

The legend seemed to try to scowl, but there was too much of a grin for it to overcome. "You have to watch out for that girl. She's trouble."

"Interesting, she gave me the same warning about you, sir."

"Then you're twice warned," the legend said, pointing Taylor to what the agent knew to be the library. The legend led him to a pair of sofas, facing each other before a fireplace that was large enough to play cards in.

On the table between them was a platter with some delicious looking confections, as well as a coffee urn and a thermos of hot water.

"What would you like to drink?" the general asked.

"Tea, please," Taylor said.

The general poured hot water into two delicately fine china cups of white with gold filigree and offered Taylor a box full of assorted teas. Taylor chose Earl Gray and began to steep his tea with purpose.

"So," the general said, dipping his own tea bag of Earl Gray, "Where is Kris?"

"You don't know?"

"I have many kids, grandkids, and more great-grandkids than I can hope to keep track of, considering that the last number keeps changing. No great-great-grandkids. That generation seems too busy to find time for kids." He paused to stare at nothing far away before adding. "Their loss."

"I thought you had seen Kris only recently," the agent found himself falling back into his professional form.

The legend easily fell back into his own form. He sipped his tea and gave away nothing.

"Pardon me. I shouldn't have asked that," Taylor said. "I am on leave, but it seems I'm to have a businessman's holiday."

That eyebrow went up, again.

Taylor took that for a nebulous question and attempted to answer some of it. "Kris is, for the moment, safe on the Musashi battleship *Mutsu*. Unfortunately, she is in custody and headed for her day in court."

The grandfather across from Taylor frowned. "Musashi still has the death penalty, doesn't it?"

"Kris told me that she was aware of that before she surrendered herself."

"Hmm," was all the grandfather offered.

After taking a moment to weigh the general's bland facade, Taylor went on. "Were you aware that Alexander Longknife had three of the upper stories of his tower ready to be flooded with Sarin gas?"

That struck a nerve.

The general scowled. "That man is going around the bend without a paddle," he growled.

"It seems so," the agent in Foile agreed. "The question is just how far around which bend he intends to go?"

The general eyed Taylor for a long moment. Taylor met him measure for measure.

"What has my great-granddaughter shared with you?" General Trouble asked.

Taylor told him in as few words as he could manage.

When he finished, the general took a final sip of his tea, set it down and fixed Taylor with a level gaze. "You're in a lot of trouble," he said.

"I'll take that as a complement, coming from you," Taylor said with an even grin.

Trouble grinned right back. Tiger to tiger.

"So," the old general said, "what do you plan to do about this?"

"I intend to find out if there is a Fleet of Fools intent on making all the mistakes Princess Kristine's Fleet of Discovery did not make," Taylor said.

"That will be a tough nut to crack," Trouble said.

"I've cracked a few tough nuts in my time," Taylor answered evenly.

"I imagine that you have. And, no hard feelings on not getting to Kris before she made her try last night."

"I am glad that I failed," Taylor admitted. "I haven't blown it very often, but if there was ever a situation where I needed to do a face plant, this was the one."

"So, assuming that you are not here to arrest me, what can I do for you?" the general said, relaxing into his sofa.

"If you were Alexander Longknife, and sending out a treasure fleet, what ship or ships would you send? If we can identify the likely ships, I can begin to look for a weak link in the crew."

Trouble rubbed at his chin. "Ships, especially merchant ships, are not my area of expertise. You might want to talk to Kris's brother, Honovi. He may be a politician, but he's a good one. As of late, he's been working on laws relating to merchant ship safety. He might know what you need to know. Then again, he might not."

"You're the second person to suggest I have a talk with him," Taylor said. "Kris did as well."

"Then let me get you an appointment to see a very busy member of parliament." Trouble said, and began making the arrangements.

3

Late that evening, Taylor Foile found himself ushered into a nursery where Member of Parliament Honovi Longknife was walking slowly back and forth, bouncing a tiny infant who seemed more colicky than happy with his father's attention.

"I'm sorry I could not see you sooner," the young father whispered, letting his infant offspring grab his little finger and hold on tight. A burp brought a smile to its tiny lips and another one to the father's.

"A new unhappy tummy?" Taylor asked.

"Terribly so," the father said. "The doctors assure us this is just a stage, but it cannot end soon enough for me."

Taylor raised a questioning eyebrow.

"My wife and I are switching off nights. Tonight, I have the duty. And yes, we do have hired help, but there are just some things a father and mother should do."

Taylor suspected that the Great Billy Longknife had had little to do with his own children's upbringing. Here was a new father in rebellion against the pattern. Maybe not as vocal and public as the young princess's, but cut from the same family tree.

The father switched to Member of Parliament as he turned his gaze from child to agent. "Grampa Trouble said you've talked to Kris and him and needed to talk to me. I'm sorry I couldn't cut some time out sooner for you, but . . ." the young man shrugged.

The movement of his shoulders was easily subsumed into this walking and bouncing of the infant, but Taylor caught it. "Is there anything I can do for you?"

"Your sister and the General think you can," Taylor said and began again to spin out the tale Kris had shared with him, cut now to the absolute fewest words. Before he was done, the scion to the Longknife throne interrupted him.

Honovi was shaking his head. "Grampa Al would never do that," leaked out in more of a yelp than a whisper. The infant, who had been starting to doze off opened his eyes to take in his surroundings, but a huge yawn of tiny proportions led to drooping eyes again.

When the infant again slept in his father's worried arms, the Member of Parliament went on in a firm whisper. "I was there the night when Grampa Al swore off politics and demanded Father do the same. Grampa Al would never get involved in politics. Certainly not off-planet."

"At least one off-planet president thinks he has, and I believe your sister has come to that conclusion as well."

The frown on the young father's face did not seem convinced, but Taylor went on with Kris's tale.

"Sarin!" came out as a whispered yelp. "My grandfather rigged that Palace of Insecurity with Sarin?"

"So I am told," Taylor said. "And when your sister left the building with a shuttle launch, there was no chance for me to check the story."

"Al had a shuttle there, too!" though whispered, lacked nothing in incredulity.

"I saw it with my own eyes. Your sister launched it to take her up to the Musashi battleship *Mutsu* where she surrendered herself to their justice."

"They still have the death penalty," sounded more like a request for him to deny the statement.

Taylor nodded. "Still. They use the axe."

"Oh, Sis, what have you gotten yourself into now?"

"Whatever it is, she did it with full knowledge."

"My sister has a death wish."

"I do not know her as well as you do, sir, but I would not agree with you."

"True. Maybe it's not a death wish. But I sure don't know what else it could be."

Taylor was dearly tempted to offer an opinion of, "A strong sense of duty," but he could see where that would take the conversation, and that was not the reason he was here.

"The general suggested that your recent work on revising the Merchant Marine Laws might give you insight into our next problem."

"There's more?"

Taylor told Honovi of Kris's fear that her grandfather was preparing to launch a Fleet of Fools.

The young father stood for a long moment, gently swaying with his babe in arms. The child seemed to be lost in the sleep of the innocent . . . who are well burped.

Kris's brother settled his new son into a bassinet, checked to make sure the child monitor was working, and motioned the agent on leave to lead him from the nursery. With one backwards glance, the Member of Parliament led Taylor down the hall to a small office.

The tan walls were in need of paint. The desk was chipped gray metal. The wall in front of it was covered with pigeon holes overflowing with data storage chips The two chairs also deserved replacement.

"Merchant ships, huh?" Honovi muttered.

"Merchant ships loaded with every good thing we make."

"Have you read the logs of the *Wasp*? Kris's ship."

"I have not heard anything about the logs of that ship. Why?" Taylor asked.

"I'm not surprised you haven't," the Member of Parliament said. "They were confiscated and shipped immediately to Wardhaven on the same courier that brought Kris back. I think Dad invented a new security classification for them. 'Slit your throat before reading' or something."

"Without divulging the content, could you tell me why they are so special?"

"They tell how Kris managed to get the jump gates to throw ships a thousand light years or more," her brother said.

The agent whistled. "I thought most jumps took you twenty or thirty light years. Fifty is considered a long jump."

"Yes," Honovi said.

"So, anyone wanting to get to the other side of the galaxy before they died would need to know what Kris did," the agent said.

"Exactly."

"So, who has read those logs?"

"Very few. Access is restricted. You have to have a 'need to know,' and not many meet Father's very restricted idea of needing to know."

The agent in Taylor stared at the ceiling. "Didn't we just install an entirely new security system for Wardhaven's net?"

"I believe so," the young man, frowning at this turn of the conversation. "Word is that it's tighter than a drum."

"Very tight. I understand that even your sister's famous Nelly was locked out."

"Serves Sis right," the brother who stayed home almost crowed.

"Who sold us this marvelous system?" Taylor asked, knowing the answer all too well.

The smile on the Member of Parliament grew grave. "My grandfather Al," he whispered through a scowl.

Taylor canted his head to study the flow of emotions racing across the young man's face. It finished with a soft groan and a muttered, "How much do you want to bet me that the access log on that file is missing one or two entries?"

"No bet," the agent said.

"No bet," the young man echoed. "But it won't do him all that much good," he said, with a chuckle. "Al has been pushing us to cut the regulations and red tape that affect the merchant fleet. He's been hammering on us for the last five years to lighten up on the power requirements for ships. Shippers can make more money if their ships have only the reactors and motors they need to make .85 gees acceleration or deceleration. Cut down on the deadweight of the ship and it can carry more cargo at a lower price. Also, if we change the laws so the ships don't have to carry extra reaction mass from port to port, again he makes more money."

Hanovi paused, then added. "Of course, you have a damn thin safety margin if things go sideways."

The agent raised a questioning eyebrow.

The Member of Parliament leaned back and eyed the ceiling as he explained. "Most major shipping lanes begin and end at space stations with reaction mass for sale. 'Why should ships have to lug around more hydrogen for more jumps than there are between their scheduled ports? Weight costs money,' Al kept yammering at me. 'Let ships get by with no more reaction mass than they need and no more power plant than is necessary to get from port to port. We can build ships for specific trade routes and cut the price to the bare minimum'."

"But," Taylor was quick to point out, "that will make the ship very dependent on ports and very specialized for that route."

"Exactly," Honovi agreed. "Planets that don't provide enough trade for their own specially built fleet will be sloughed off to general ships at a higher price."

"And if you wanted to go jumping around the galaxy using this new technique your sister discovered...?"

"You'd need a whole different bunch of ships. Totally new design with more power and a whole lot more storage tanks for reaction mass. Probably stronger hull scantlings, too, though I can't tell you why without having to slit your throat."

The two men stared at each other, a tight smile growing on their faces.

"So," Taylor said, "What type of merchant ships are they building at the Nuu yards up on the station at this very minute?"

"Very specialized ones, if you believe what my grandfather tells me. But," Honovi said, raising a finger, "I don't believe everything Al tells me. I have my contacts at the yards and among the merchant skippers. Let me make a few calls tomorrow."

"And I do not doubt that someone I know will know someone who is very good at getting around this new net security," Taylor said.

"Who?" Honovi asked.

"Your sister did not get as high as she did in Al's tower without knowing something about the layout. *She* had just arrived back on Wardhaven. Someone must have provided her with her intel."

"Who?" the brother repeated.

"I will be talking to General Tordon again tomorrow morning."

"Who else but Grampa Trouble?" Honovi agreed, a loving scowl on his face for his rascal of a great grandfather.

4

At 8:30 am, Foile was again knocking on the front door to Nuu House.

Without so much as a request for identification, the legend himself answered. "I was expecting you. Care for breakfast?" he asked.

They adjourned to the kitchen where Taylor found himself sharing a breakfast of huge and wide-ranging proportions.

"Do you do this every day?" Taylor asked.

"Of course not," Trouble chuckled. "But a brunch starts at 0930 for an immense number of Honovi's closest friends. Fortunate for us, we can mooch before they arrive."

The breakfast was quite enjoyable. It turned out that the cook's husband was a veteran, invalided out of the service after the Unity War nearly ninety years ago. He and Trouble began swapping war stories that couldn't possibly be true, but raised the hairs on the back of Taylor's neck, nonetheless.

Only when the cook and her husband began setting up the brunch did Taylor have a moment to pose a question to

Trouble of how he might gain a better grasp of who had accessed the *Wasp's* logs.

"And why do you think I might know of some such wizard?" the legend said, eyeing the agent in a fashion that likely would have a normal human crawling under the table.

Taylor ignored the urge, but did take the time to consider how he might broach the topic without becoming an accessory after the fact to Kris's little breaking and entering expedition. Failing to find a way around it, Taylor chose to ignore it.

"Let me simply say, without laying a basis for my suspicion, that I think you know someone with the prerequisite skills."

"Spoken like a cautious man who knows his way around the law," the old general replied with a chuckle. "Let me contemplate a few of my sins and see who I might recommend to you. Recommend to you without any surety of success since, I, no doubt, have never used their services."

"No doubt at all," Taylor said, lying through his teeth with just as much feigned innocence.

A moment later, the cook returned but didn't head for the stove. "Honovi slipped this to me and said to see that you got it. How'd he know you were here?"

Taylor shrugged. He was getting way too good at avoiding saying what he knew. *When I get back to the office after this vacation, will I need another one to regain my reputation for probity?*

When they were again alone, Taylor opened the note. It had a number scrawled across it that had just the right numerics to be a phone number.

The general raised a questioning eyebrow as Taylor had his computer run the number in a reverse search. It was the personal number of a structural engineer working for Nuu Yard up on the station.

The general allowed Taylor a smile. "Good kid, Honovi is. Add this number to your list," he said and slipped a phone number across the table.

Again, Taylor ran the number through the directory. This time the reaction was NUMBER NOT IN USE.

"Surprised?" Taylor asked.

"Not at all," Trouble assured him.

"It seems that I have my work cut out for me," Taylor said, pushing back from the table.

"Or at least a start," the general said, raising to his feet and offering Taylor his hand.

"May I get back to you when I have more to report?" Taylor asked.

"I'm hardly in your chain of command," the general answered.

"For this particular case, you are the closest person I have to that role."

"So, if you are Kris Longknife's bloodhound, what would that make me?"

"Have you ever been Master of the Hunt?"

"Hunts for Iteeche maybe. Never for the truth. It's far too illusive for the likes of me."

"Well, I have never worked for a princess either."

"Well then," Trouble said, "let us see if we old dogs can learn a few new tricks."

5

Taylor called the number Trouble had given him. Surprise of surprises, it took him to a voice box that did not ask him to leave a message. Still, the agent left his name and number and managed not to cringe too much as he said, "Trouble sent me."

Honovi's number called for more consideration. Again, Taylor found himself going up the beanstalk. This time, he headed for the area outside the Nuu yard. There, he easily found the Lost Dutchman. It was a huge eatery of no particular ambiance. Clearly, it was intended to get a lot of hungry folks fed with a minimum of fuss. It offered a breakfast menu before the first and second shift, a lunch menu in the middle of both and a supper menu when either was done.

Taylor arrived an hour before the end of the day shift. He found a public net access and called the number.

"Yeah," came harried but quick.

"Honovi Longknife suggested I talk to you," was all Taylor said.

"About what?" was laden with caution.

"This and that," sounded vague enough for Taylor.

"Where?"

"The Lost Dutchman sound good to you?"

"How will I know you?"

"I'll be in the back, and I'll know you." Taylor's directory included a picture of the woman. Taylor had not enabled the video of his borrowed net access.

"You're lucky. It doesn't look like I'll have to work late," was followed quickly by a click.

Taylor ordered himself a lemonade and downloaded the latest copy of **Jane's All the Worlds' Merchant Ships**. After realizing the standard version was little more than a recognition manual with the bare minimum of specs on the ships, he paid for the attached database that included builders as well as the full specs on the power plants and other technical data.

It was the technical data he most wanted to know.

First, Taylor arranged the data by newest construction to oldest. Honovi was correct. Ships delivered most recently were different from those five years ago. Fully loaded with cargo, they were much larger than the earlier ones, yet, their power plants were a good third less powerful than those for the older ships. When he compared empty deadweight to fully loaded mass, the ratio was a good twenty to thirty percent higher.

Taylor stared off into the middle distance of the large dining room as he worked to connect the dots. The new hulls must be a lot lighter. They also likely contained fewer or smaller storage tanks for reaction mass. Honovi had been careful to reveal nothing about the content of the *Wasp's* log, but he'd been definite that these jumps involved hard accelerations and that meant well reinforced hulls, big reactors, and plenty of reaction mass to feed them.

New construction might make it to the next port with no problems, but a thousand-light year jump? Not so likely.

Taylor turned back to his database. "What can you tell me about new construction?"

According to one of the advertisements that came with the database, the Nuu Yards were producing a new class of ships. They were huge, light, and low powered. "The most economical trade ships for the new age," it bragged.

Taylor reviewed the specs for the *Pride of Free Enterprise*, and the *Pride of the Free Market*. They were light as a prima ballerina and likely just as beautiful . . . and highly specialized.

After staring at them for a long minute, Taylor tapped for the update option on the page. It cost, but promised to give him the most up to date information on the construction of the ships and the latest press releases from the building yard.

A bit more than a month ago, the yard had announced that these ships would be made with the latest Smart Metal^{TM}.

"That's interesting. Why use smart metal for a merchant ship specialized for one specific trade route? Why pay for the option to reorganize your ship when you've designed it down to the last fine point to be just exactly what you want?" Taylor muttered to himself.

He strongly suspected he knew the answer.

He scrolled down for the very latest updates.

He didn't have to scroll much. There hadn't been an update in over a month. There was no launch date, nor data on any changes to the design. The latter was understandable. It was harder, however, to believe that the yard's PR had nothing to brag about concerning the first Smart

Metal™ hulls. As a point of fact, it was only slightly short of unbelievable.

Taylor closed down his net access. He needed to think about what his research showed before he talked with someone who knew just exactly what was going on, but had likely been told to forget it the moment she set foot outside her office.

On a stray thought, Taylor paid for access to **Jane's All the Worlds' Fighting Ships.**

No surprise, the USS *Wasp* had its own entry, although the final notation said the ship was being scrapped at High Chance Station. It was the earlier entries Taylor found interesting. The ship had started life as a single reactor, something that quickly found its way into the pirate trade. Captured by Princess Longknife, it came into U.S. hands after being condemned by a court on Chance.

Taylor had to pause for a moment to smile. "So, Princess, your ship began life at Chance and is now ending there. Poetry anyone?"

Since the universe did not answer, Taylor went on.

Once in the US Navy, it had been subjected to an overhaul that amounted to little short of a rebuild. It acquired a second reactor and four 18-inch pulse lasers. Its size increased so it could carry more shipping containers. Those containers had proven most versatile, carrying scientific equipment as well as quarters for the scientists. The *Wasp* had been classified as an Exploration Corvette. Oh, more containers had been added to support a Marine detachment, then more to support more Sailors who supported more of just about everything.

"Princess, I do believe your ship just kind of grew."

The pictures in the file showed the ship as it grew more and more containers. It was a boxy looking ship, but even with the largest collection it had when it departed with the Fleet of Discovery, it had been a compact looking affair.

Taylor flipped back to the displacement of the refitted corvette. Its deadweight showed it pretty solid. Even with its containers, it was still quite heavy.

"Computer, compare the tonnage of the U.S.S. *Wasp* with the tonnage of a similar freighter with the same number of shipping containers."

The computer found four small freighters. Fully loaded, they still massed well below the *Wasp*.

"There are containers for shipping computer components, and then there are containers for shipping scientists and Marines," the agent muttered to himself.

"Computer, can you find any specs for the containers the Navy is using for its ships?"

"No, sir," came back fast, but not as a surprise.

The *Wasp* had not been outfitted to make a profit, but to take a princess where she wanted to go. To let her see what she wanted to see, and get her out of any trouble she got into while there.

Taylor pushed himself back from the table and stared off into space for a long, long time.

He almost failed to notice that the restaurant was filling with after shift customers. When he did, he had little trouble spotting his engineer. She was the only lone individual looking around for someone.

Taylor had his computer do a quick visual check to verify the woman was indeed the one he'd called, then waved at her.

The woman exuded caution as he approached Taylor's table. The agent stood and offered his hand.

"I am Taylor Foile. Honovi suggested I talk with you."

The woman took his hand. The shake was tentative and

calculated, perfect for an uncomfortable engineer. "I'm Annie Smedenhoff. Yes, Honovi called and said I should talk to you. Why?"

"The Prime Minister's son didn't tell you?" Why wasn't Taylor surprised?

"How much of your life do you trust to the net, Mr. Foile?" the engineer shot back. "Especially after the latest upgrade of what they call 'security'?"

"I'll concede the point. After all, I'm here talking to you in person. Do you trust we *can* talk here?"

The young woman pulled a thin pink box from her purse, punched the single, green button on its face and set it in the middle of the table. A moment later, Taylor noticed two small, glowing dust motes.

"Yes, I think we can talk," the woman said.

"Were you followed by, ah, them?" Taylor asked.

"No telling, but now, no doubt, they will not be telling, will they? By the way, I'm recording this conversation. Are you?"

Taylor had not expected this level of paranoia. However, he'd been warned enough that he was venturing onto dangerous ground if he tried to follow the Longknife princess's question.

"On official business, yes, I do. However, as it turns out, I am on vacation at the moment," Taylor said, as he reached into his pocket and removed an old-fashioned pad of paper and pen. "Today, I may take notes on the more complex issues in your area of technical expertise."

"So, Member of Parliament Honovi Longknife calls me up and asks me to meet with you, on your vacation, huh?"

"On my vacation, I am attempting to unravel a riddle of sorts."

"A riddle. Of sorts," Annie said, and punched for a cobb

salad on the computer menu at the table. Taylor took the moment to order a Ruben sandwich, no fries.

"Yes, a riddle. I don't know if you know, but Princess Kristine Longknife went to call on her grandfather, Alexander, a few days ago."

Annie smiled. It was a nice addition to her face. She wore no makeup except maybe a touch of lipstick. The smile added a glow to her face and a slight dimple on her left cheek. "So, that was what the commotion was all about. I knew someone at the yard had to go collect a shuttle from, what was it, the *Matsu*?"

"The Imperial Musashi Battleship *Mutsu*," Taylor corrected.

"Yes," she said, and Taylor had the distinct impression he had passed a test of sorts.

"The shuttle is being refurbished down to the glue on its skin. I understand it will then be returned to Mr. Alexander's own Tower of Power."

Their meals arrived on a self-propelled trolley. They removed their food. Foile settled up their tab with cash and the trolley rolled off.

"You are, ah, seeking your privacy," Annie said.

"What privacy I may have. No doubt, there are cameras recording our presence in the room."

"But there is too much ambient noise for them to separate our conversation from so many others, at least at the moment.

A few feet away, another dust mote glowed bright for a moment, then dissipated.

"The Longknife princess went to extremes to talk to her grandfather," Taylor said, going straight to the point. No doubt, their conversation would have to be over all too soon.

Sad that, because Annie was a pleasant woman to spend time with.

"And what did she want to talk to her grandfather about?" Annie said, taking a bite of her salad.

"Is he thinking of sending freighters out beyond human space?"

"Oh," Annie said. She swallowed her mouthful, took another bite and finished chewing it without saying another word.

Taylor ignored his sandwich. "I have pulled up all the information available about the ships now building in the Nuu Yards. I know that they are Smart Metal, a strange and expensive choice for ships intended to spend their lifetime plying the well-ordered shipping lanes between comfortable point A and profitable point B. Honovi also sees this as strange. He thought you might tell us something since, despite the Nuu Yards' usually verbose press releases, there has been nothing in them about the *Pride of Free Enterprise* for the last six weeks."

She took another bite, while staring at the wall to the right of Taylor's face.

When she finally spoke, her words came very softly. Taylor had to work hard to hear them over the talk at the nearby tables. "There won't be any press releases, even when they're launched, take on their first cargo, and depart on their first voyage."

"That's unusual," Taylor said, equally softly.

"Unheard of," Annie corrected him. "Totally unheard of. Nuu Yards never misses a chance to herald the wheels of progress. At least, not until these two ships came along."

"What's so strange about them?" Taylor asked.

"They're gigantic!" Annie said. "We've added the two reactors for the next two ships on to them. Four in each hull.

Huge engines, and plenty of them. Also, we're pouring the Smart Metal from the next planned ships into these two. That might just mean that someone wants to ship a whole lot of stuff, but that can't be all of it."

"Why?"

Again, she paused, but not to take another bite. Now, she was arranging all the croutons in the salad in a line on the right side of the plate.

"There is no way for an uninformed engineer to know anything about the potential use a ship will be put to," she said. "However, engineers are not blind. You ask us to do something, we can't help but extrapolate the data to its logical conclusions. The conclusion may originate in sales, but they are, surprisingly often, logical. Particularly if they intend to turn a profit. And Alexander may be many things, but he never has his eyes far from the bottom line."

Taylor took this rambling conversation for something that would lead to somewhere. He did not interrupt. He was quickly rewarded for his forbearance.

"I've been asked to calculate the longitudinal hull strength members needed to bear up to 2.5 gees, and to pass my calculations along to the Smart Metal programmers so they can develop a standard configuration using that acceleration. That is unusual acceleration for a merchant ship, don't you think?"

"Yes, considering that Mr. Longknife had been lobbying parliament for the last five years to allow for the absolute minimum of ship, reactor, and reaction mass needed to get from a specific point A to point B."

"Yes. I worked on those calculations too," Annie said, and seemed to think better of ignoring her salad. She took a bite and chewed it slowly as she went on. "What's unusual about these ships is that I've also been asked to recalculate the lateral strength members. How much cargo can the ship take on and keep aboard safely while high under centripetal forces."

"While the hull is rotating?" Taylor asked to make sure he understood.

"Yes. That's crazy. You accelerate a ship at one gee, and you've got a down equal to one gravity. Nice. That's what lines do. This station rotates at just the right speed so that the A Deck has enough centripetal force that you feel like it's one gravity. Nice. Mix the two up and you get one hell of a confused inner ear."

The two stared at each other.

"It makes no sense," the young woman said.

"It has to make sense," Taylor said. Something was gnawing at the back of his mind.

"Wait a second," he said and called up the **Fighting Ships** database. He'd flipped through the first couple of entries before he'd launched a search for the *Wasp*. Now he went back to those early entries. They showed the fleet of Earth. Battleships had pride of place.

"Look at these battleships. Have you ever worked on the design of one of them?" he asked the engineer.

"No. Not even in college. They're obsolete. No one has built one since the Iteeche War. There are scads of them left over from then." She paused for a moment. "Well, almost no one. There are reports that Greenfield has built a few of them. They didn't do much in the war and they don't have all the relics in orbit that most of us have. Anyway. No, I've never worked on something like that. Corvettes, destroyers. Yes, we make them."

"Look at the notation on these battleships. What's 15 RPM mean? This one is 20 RPM."

"Revolutions per minute." Annie spoke the words as if

from pure rote, something she had memorized long ago but saw no application here.

Then she shook her head. "You don't rotate a ship. The *Santa Maria*, one of the first exploration starships launched from Earth, did a bad jump because it had a bad thruster and took on a rotation as it did its first jump. They ended up way across the galaxy. It took another ship on a bad jump to find it."

"How'd that happen?"

"You must have read about it. Ray Longknife's ship was sabotaged. We never did find out who did it. Anyway, he and his ship ended up way the hell and gone and stumbled onto the lost colony the crew of the *Santa Maria* had set up. At least the survivors. All I know is that we engineers design ships to stay steady as rocks when we approach a jump."

"So, why do these battleships advertise how many revolutions per minute they can do?" Taylor asked. Now he knew why you didn't want to do RPMs. He still didn't know why these particular ships did them.

"Oh," Annie said, and Taylor could almost see a light bulb above her head light up. "Lasers. These battleships have thick ice armor. See, three meters thick. Three and a half for this big bruiser. That's to absorb laser hits."

"So?" Taylor said, still not enlightened.

"Even with that much ice, if you hit it with a big enough laser, it will melt through, so they rotate the ship to force any laser hits to burn through more ice. It creates a hell of a problem keeping the ships balanced. You burn off some armor on a fast rotating ship, and you've got the devil's own time keeping your ship from spinning itself to destruction. Now, I remember this problem in class. A classic first year problem. How fast do you need to redistribute reaction mass and how much pumping power do you need? I aced it." she said with a proud smile.

"Are they asking you to figure out how much pumping power you'll need to redistribute weight on this rotating ship?" Taylor asked.

"No. No one's raised that problem. I wonder if I should."

"Please don't do it tomorrow," Taylor suggested, trying to sound as helpful as he might.

"Yeah. Right."

"So, let's see what have we have here," Taylor reflected. "Merchant ships that are huge, and, unlike everything that was put forward for the last five years, have excessive power plants. They also are designed for higher gee and we have this RPM issue, but no thought of armor."

"No. We're not putting ice armor on them, though I did overhear some folks at lunch from the Navy side of the yard talking about having the new Smart Metal do its own rotation thing. With this new stuff, we can get it spinning around on the outer skin of the ship without the crew inside having to spin with it. It will even redistribute itself as it takes hits. Fantastic stuff! Oh, but you didn't hear that from me."

"Hear what?" Taylor said, allowing himself a small but friendly smile. "As a matter of fact, I haven't heard anything." Then he frowned. "Anything that I can connect the dots to."

Annie took another bite from her salad. "I think there is one more dot for your little puzzle."

"Yes?"

Again, she chewed her food. "There is a third ship we are working on. It's small and has to be ready when the big two are launched."

"A third, small ship?"

"Yes, little, but not normally little. It has three smaller reactors. Normally, you try to fit the reactor to the ship. Small ship, small reactor. Big ship, bigger reactor. If you get big enough, you add a second reactor. That's what is economical. You don't ever put three of the smallest size ones on one ship."

"Redundancy?" Taylor guessed.

"That's all I can figure out. It's also small and not at all rigged for cargo. In fact, it's not rigged for much of anything. The programmer working on the Smart Metal configurations of the ship has gotten huge bonuses, but other than him showing off pictures of his new sports car, he's not saying a word about his work."

"A small ship but with redundant power plants so that if one went down on a long voyage you'd still have the other two. Is there anything else special about it?"

"It's getting the same sensor suite that the big ships are getting. That includes a Mark XII rangefinder."

"How is that special?"

"It's just the best and most expensive rangefinder on the market, and Westinghouse charges an arm and a leg for them."

"Just a second," Taylor said, and called up the entry on the *Wasp*. "Yes, it got one of the first Mark XII rangefinders. It was installed just before Kris Longknife found those two planets loaded with alien artifacts out past Chance. There's a tight control over who gets to go there and how they go. Strange, a pot of gold at the end of the rainbow and no one's beating a trail there," Taylor mused.

"Strange, that," was all Annie said.

"I take it that you know a lot more than I do."

"Very likely, but it doesn't involve what that Longknife girl is up to lately, so let's not go there."

"Are you putting big lasers on these ships so that they need the best rangefinder?"

"That's just it. All three ships have no armament. As I understand it, there won't even be a gun locker, although with Smart Metal, you can change that real fast."

"Stranger and stranger," Taylor said. He glanced down at his notebook. He'd totally forgotten to take notes. He scrawled Mark XII and left it at that.

"Well, I do have a date with my cat and some good TV tonight," Annie said, applying a napkin to her mouth. "It's been a ball sharing my ignorance with you. If you ever find yourself in my neck of the woods not knowing anything and wanting to know even less, look me up. You have my number."

Taylor chuckled at her joke, and stood like a gentleman as she left. He sat down and made some more notes. He reviewed several of the pages in his two databases, then slowly ate his sandwich. He obviously knew a lot of interesting stuff that related to each other in some rational way.

The only problem was, he didn't know enough about the entire puzzle to see how they fit together.

Sandwich finished, he stood up, signaled a wandering trolley and bussed his own table. As he did so, he noticed a man standing in the doorway of the restaurant, eyeing him.

"Computer, who is that man?" Taylor whispered.

"There is a 97.382 percent probability that he is Arlen Cob, a senior investigator with Nuu Security, assigned to Nuu High Wardhaven Station Docks."

When Taylor reached the door, Arlen was gone. Midway to the space elevator station, and with no apparent tail, Taylor attached to the transient net and called Honovi, leaving a cryptic note that he hoped the busy young man would take for a request to meet with him again for some quality baby time. He also found an even more cryptic note from the number that was not in use at this time. A woman's voice asked him to meet her at a place near his office. She used the unique name the regulars applied to it, something that brought a smile to cops, but meant nothing to most civilians.

Taylor increased his pace towards the beanstalk station.

6

The Atrium was many places, organized around a hollow square that rose nine floors to a clear ceiling. There were trees and vines twining green around stairwells and elevators between the floors. Every once in a while, it seemed to rain, but it was a fine mist and only fell where the plants needed it.

A well-managed jungle, the cops called it. While people with too much money spent it among the greenery of the nine floors, the basement had several nice places were working folks might hang out. Government types, with only the pay voters saw fit to give them.

Taylor would bet money that his caller didn't intend to meet him in the basement. The voice was too well manicured.

He took a seat at a finely worked cast iron table and pulled out his reader. He was way behind on his comic strips. Mostly, he stayed to the strips that did their jokes in a day. He could never count on following a storyline that covered a week, much less a month. He caught up on the last week of his favorites, then turned to the one long plotted comic he enjoyed. He had to flip back through six weeks before he could find the beginning of this particular story arc and follow the jokes. Taylor was smiling happily at a particularly good running line of jokes when the woman who had sent him here entered.

At least, he hoped she was looking for him.

Likely, well over half the eyes in the Atrium followed her, hoping she had come to meet them. While engineer Annie had fit in, using light makeup and a shirt and pants that were nearly the uniform of the civilian workforce, this woman stood out.

Her dress was clearly professional, but the tight sheath of several competing shades of gray drew the eye and made every step she took a celebrating of several million years of female evolution and locomotion. Her makeup turned a lovely face into something striking and unforgettable.

Clearly, today she's not afraid to be remembered. *I wonder what she looks like when she doesn't want to be so memorable?* the professional in Taylor thought.

As she passed his table she spoke softly, "Agent Foile, will you walk with me?"

He pocketed his reader and rose to follow her. In a moment, he was beside her. "No agent today. I'm on vacation."

"I am rarely asked to go fishing," the woman said. "I really doubt you are on holiday."

Taylor chose not to press the point.

They entered an elevator and the woman pressed for nine. Taylor had staked out a few stores on that level. Most of them sold the most expensive works of art on Wardhaven. However, she led him to a small restaurant.

"Your usual, Mademoiselle M?"

"Certainly, Charles."

"It's ready for you," was all the maître d' said.

Without looking back, Mademoiselle M led Taylor to a small room with a table and chairs. She held the door open for him to enter, then closed it firmly behind her. The room was something Tailor had only heard of. Art work in gold frames, rich cream wallpaper with gold filigree running through it in a flower pattern, and a plush blue carpet enveloped his shoes.

"Clear," the woman said and suddenly all the falderal vanished. The walls were Spartan white and bare of anything. The table, chairs and carpet were still there, but Taylor had seen interrogation rooms with more warmth than this room now exuded.

He took a chair. She settled into the chair across from him. From her small purse, she removed a compact and began to check her makeup. She was careful to keep the mirror out of Taylor's line of sight.

The agent would bet money that the "compact" was doing a far more thorough check of the security of this room than Annie's pink box had done.

"So, how is your vacation going, Mr. Foile?" she said. The tone was chit chat.

Taylor chose to return the soft ball with an equally easy pitch. "So far, I'm just in the decompression stage. I usually need a week just to shake off the stress of the job. I was catching up on the last month of comics when you walked by."

She put the compact away.

"So why are we here?"

"Trouble sent me."

"He only sends me trouble. What kind of trouble are you, Mr. Senior Chief Agent in Charge? You still licking the wounds from your chase after Kris Longknife?"

"I didn't know that made the news."

"It didn't. I rarely bother with the official version. No, I was following you and her antics on your Bureau net. You would have had a better chance of catching her if you knew where she was headed."

"Ah, but I didn't. My orders to 'Find her before she gets herself and others killed,' was rather vague."

"Which leaves one to wonder if you were intended to fail?" she said, raising a perfectly arched eyebrow.

"If I was to fail, why send me?"

"Yes." she said. "So, why did Trouble send me to you?"

"It seems that the logs of the *Wasp's* last voyage, it being the princess's flag, were brought back to Wardhaven and buried under an entirely new security level. 'Burn After Reading,' or some such thing. The question posed to me by a good friend was whether or not we can trust the access logs of the data, or have the travels of our wayward princess been read more widely than the Prime Minister would prefer."

The woman shook her head. "If you don't want data read, don't put it on the net. Back in the ancient days, the only way to access some data was to place an order to have the tapes hung on the computer. You did what you wanted, then put them back in a locked box, or so my old grandmother insists. It wasn't that way in her day, but in her great-grandmother's day, no doubt, when the dinosaurs stomped the Earth."

She paused to enjoy Taylor's smile at her humor. "Who has these logs?"

"I don't know. They are Navy property, I would suspect that the Navy has custody of them."

"Hmm." Now Taylor observed that even a frown looked good on her. "That could definitely complicate my job. The Navy types are notoriously untrusting. They insisted on being trained up on this new security system and then tweaked it to their liking. I could likely walk into the Prime Minister's personal files without him twitching to the visit. Navy, ah, not so much."

She paused to study her fingernails for a long moment. They were a most stunning shade of lavender, and matched her eyeshadow. Taylor had seen the combination on teenagers and been tempted to ship them off to the morgue.

On her, it was strangely alluring.

Or was it that, on her, even death would be alluring. Taylor closed down that line of thought. Hard.

"To get somewhere, it often helps to know where you are coming from. Do you have any guess who these pairs of unauthorized eyes might belong to?"

"Some of Mr. Alexander Longknife's associates," Taylor said.

Mademoiselle M uttered a nasty word. "Why should I risk my neck, as well as my street cred on some intramural dust-up between that family?" she snapped, and glanced at the door.

Taylor suspected that she might allow him one more sentence. Maybe two.

"The life of all humanity just may be weighing in the balance."

"Says who?" she snarled.

"Kris Longknife. And Trouble seems to agree with her."

"That girl. Maybe. Him? Damn. Start talking, Mr. Taylor. I might have bought your pig in a poke for just an ordinary problem. This has got foul smelling stuff all over it and very likely several pounds of explosives thrown in for a joke."

Quickly, Taylor ran the woman through the runaround the Longknifes had subjected him to, from chasing Kris Longknife for her father to the daughter charging him to get to the bottom of why the grandfather was so allergic to talking to his offspring."

"He popped Sarin gas in his own office and ran away, long dress hauled up to show his bare ass," the woman snapped as Foile ended his story.

"I was told about the Sarin and did not have the opportunity to observe him in full retreat,"

"I would have done this just for just the pictures of that," she said. "Why are these logs suddenly so interesting to the old man?"

"They may contain just how Kris Longknife managed to make long jumps. Jumps of thousands of light years."

"Right. I wondered how she managed to get there and back again before the onset of menopause. And if he has read the method to her madness?"

"He may dispatch a trade fleet full of all the best goodies we make to see if he can be more successful in opening negotiations with these aliens."

The lovely lady said another, nastier word. "Some men just never understand that 'no' means 'no', and 'no way in hell' means 'no, you can't,' really."

The two could easily agree on that.

"Okay, if Trouble sent you, then he shares the same fear that Kris Longknife does. You said you were on vacation. I take that to mean that I can't send a bill to that nice slush fund that the WBI usually pays me out of when they need my services."

"I doubt it."

"And if I am hauled in, sporting handcuffs, no one is likely to loan me a key when others aren't looking?"

"If we succeed, there is likely to be a nice plaque attesting to the gratitude of a grateful nation. Otherwise, we may both rot in jail for the rest of our lives."

"Which won't be long, because the monsters will come and kill us all."

"I like working with an optimist," Taylor said, smiling.

She reached across the table and removed a small bit of lint from his coat and crushed it between her fingers. "I wonder how long that has been there?" she said.

"I have my standard issue bug detector in my pocket," he said.

"Standard issue," she made sound like an even nastier word.

"Has someone been listening in to our entire conversation?"

"Of course not. I squelched the transmitter on that puppy before I said hello. I was wondering whether it might be worth my while to let you continue passing worthless stuff to whomever is interested in you. I just decided I don't want to."

"How long has it been there?" Taylor asked, not at all liking the taste in his mouth left by the idea of him being a pawn in someone else's chase.

"Hard to tell. We can make them so tiny, but they still need power. The smaller they are, the shorter the time they can transmit anything. Then, of course, they might record and only send late at night. Who knows. Where have you been?"

Which was an easy way for her to get a list of just who was playing in this game. He tried to stay vague, but she got the gist. "The Prime Minister's residence is no big show.

They really need to hire me to clean up their act. Nuu house is fine. I check their security once a month. Sooner, if I think they need it. The engineer you met up on the station. What did her box look like?"

Taylor used his fingers to give the measurements of the device. "Pink with a light green button. More than that, I cannot say."

"It sounds like a Private Eyes Only, which can mean nothing at all if you don't actually set the thing up."

"She seemed security minded," Taylor said.

"We shall see." She rummaged in her purse, muttering softly to herself. "No, not the compact, it would take too long to train the poor fellow. Oh, right," she said, and pulled a small ball from her purse. Besides being round, it swirled with a rainbow of colors, ever changing, like a miniature gas giant planet.

"Here, keep this in your pocket."

"What is it?"

"A talisman. A magic charm. Call it what you will, but it should ward off the evil electronic bugs for the next week."

Taylor held it up to the light and watched the eddies and swirls within it. "Will it jam my own system? I'm not totally ignorant of modern life. I don't eat with my toes."

"No doubt that you are and no doubt that you don't," the woman said, seeming to enjoy his joke. "Now, you go your way and I will go mine. I'll get back to you when I have something to share with you." Mademoiselle M rose from her chair.

Taylor rose too, as a gentleman should and said, "Then I may just go fishing until I have something to share with you."

"Oh, where do you like to toss in your hook?"

Taylor chose to ignore the double entendre and

answered the simple question. "The long pier where the Severn meets the ocean."

"Oh, I often fish there. We might run into each other."

"I'll look forward to meeting you again."

"Let's hope you're not getting my one phone call from jail," she said and let him leave the room first.

7

That evening, Taylor found himself knocking on Honovi Longknife's door, again. The butler let him in and ushered him upstairs. He passed the open nursery door; tonight, the wife was doing troubled tummy duty. The infant seemed less fussy in his mother's arms.

Taylor had always envied the way his wife was able to quiet their children. A glare that would silence the most hardened criminal went right past his crying offspring.

Life was not fair.

The Member of Parliament was in his small home office. The butler knocked, announced him merely as Taylor, and left. After a "come in," Taylor opened the door and entered. The room, if anything, was more disheveled than last night. The politician had several readers open on the desk and was intently studying an old fashioned monitor.

"I hope your day was better than mine," the Member of Parliament said curtly, not taking his eyes from the screen.

"Mine was interesting," Taylor answered with intentional vagueness.

"Don't call Annie again," Honovi said, turning his chair to face Taylor. "She's spooked. Do you know she passed a Nuu Yard security type on the way out of the Lost Dutchman?"

"Yes, I saw him too. However, he was gone by the time I left. I suspect that it is his job to hang over the door like a vulture to scare anyone who might be considering anything not in his boss's interests."

"Well, whatever he was doing there, he scared the bejesus out of her. If you need to talk to anyone at the dock yard, I'll give you another contact."

"Do you have a date for the launching and fitting out of the *Pride of Free Enterprise*?"

"No, and that bothers me. Usually, I get invitations to attend those things. Maybe it's because I'm a shareholder. More likely, they want to get photos of a Member of Parliament at one of their shindigs. Anyway, I'm always told two months in advance. I can't believe it will take them more than two months to finish those ships. There are Navy ships spinning out at the yard that are taking less time than these."

"What do you know about the redesign of these ships?"

Honovi leaned forward, resting his elbows on his knees, and gave Taylor a blank stare. Taylor spent the next couple of minutes describing how the ships now had double the reactors and likely double the Smart Metal™.

Taylor concluded by saying, "I'll bet you my pension that the Kris Longknife maneuver at jump points involves high accelerations, high speeds, and high rotation on the hulls, something that is anathema among safe and rational star travelers."

"Say much more and I'll have to slit your throat," was the Member of Parliament's quiet response.

So, Taylor mentioned the Mark XII fire control system that had no lasers to call the shots for and the small tender that was also due to complete at the same time as the other two.

"A small ship?" said a surprised shareholder.

"Made of Smart Metal and with three small reactors when anyone worried about making a profit would have gone for one large one."

Honovi leaned back in his chair and eyed the ceiling. When he spoke, it was soft and thoughtful. "The *Wasp* almost wrecked herself trying to cloud dance for fuel. Their tanks were just about bone dry by then and if they couldn't get more reaction mass, they were not coming home. Really bad time my sis got herself into."

"And a Smart Metal tender," Taylor went on, "might be just what they'd need to refuel the big ships."

"Yep. That pretty much settles it. Those two oversize freighters are not headed for any planet's space station."

"And the Mark XII rangefinders?" Taylor asked.

"You really are asking me to slit your throat."

"Your father gave me crumbs to chase down Kris Longknife. I found her, too late to stop her from invading your grandfather's tower, but just in time to keep her from stepping off an elevator into a room full of Sarin gas. I would prefer to solve this mystery in time for you to stop these ships from leaving human space."

The Member of Parliament nodded along with Taylor as he made his case. When he finished, Honovi sighed.

"You make a strong argument for yourself."

"I make the only case I can."

"Okay, it's your funeral," and he quickly told the special agent what he already had figured out. "The Mark XII is the final argument that Grampa Al wants to go way off the reservation. It's the only system sensitive enough to spot what Nelly names 'fuzzy jumps.' You go through one of them just right and you're guaranteed a long jump."

"And the small tender will refuel them when they are far from the proper facilities a freighter has come to need," Taylor concluded.

"Yep. My grandpa is up to no good. Way far away up to no good."

"Now the question is: when and where? It would help if we knew who he was going to use to crew those ships and what he planned to take with him," Taylor mused.

"Who may be a function of how, which we know. Kris has insisted on surrounding herself with a young bunch, and Grampa Ray has gone along with her. Or I should say her crews are young or very fit. She tends to honk her ships around a lot, and I suspect this high rotation through a jump at high acceleration is bound to be hard on anyone who's settled into a sedate middle age."

"So, those with a beer-belly paunch need not apply?"

Honovi nodded.

"I'll have to get a list of potential sailors and check them out for physical fitness."

"That would be my first cut," the Member of Parliament agreed.

"I'll get back with you when I have something to report or need more information from you," Taylor said coming to his feet, "but for now, I think it's time for this man to take his holiday off to the fishing pier."

"You fish?"

"Metaphorically, always. As a matter of real hook, line, and sinker, not nearly enough."

"Then good fishing to you. I wish I could go along. I

don't remember the last time I took a real holiday. Father is a slave driver."

"And politics is a game without time-outs or decent rules," Taylor said.

"What I'd give for a referee or umpire."

On that shared laugh, they parted ways.

8

Taylor actually got to spend time with his own children the next morning. He let his wife sleep late and got them off to school himself. After an even later morning breakfast with her, he made his way to the fishing pier.

He invited her to come, as he always did, and she declined, as she always did. "If you catch anything, you clean it before you set foot inside this house."

At the pier, he rented a tackle box and reel from a small shop run by retirees. They seemed to be more in the business of talking about fishing and the weather, than in making money. Taylor often considered that he might work at the shop one day a week when he retired. His wife would likely appreciate the break.

For the next hour, he cast his lot to the sea, and got little back in return but empty hooks. He suspected the fish around the pier were getting too smart for the usual lures. He was just starting to consider using something from the bottom of his tackle box, something with an official suggestion that it be used in fast running mountain streams. After all, why was it in the box in the first place, and how many fish around the pier had ever passed through a fast running mountain stream?

"Hey, boss, I got something for you," said Special Agent Leslie Chu as she came up beside him and leaned on the rail.

"A fish?" he said, not looking her way.

"Nope, you're supposed to be the fisherman today, how's it going?" she said, her own eyes on the water lapping the pier supports.

"Not a bite."

"Sorry about that. I've got a few things that might interest you."

"In return for that autographed picture of Princess Kris Longknife?"

"Partial payment, at best. Did she really mean that she was sorry she missed me?"

"With a sparkle in her eye as she wrote it."

"Damn, I wish I could have been there," one of the charter members, no doubt, of the Kris Longknife fan club said with a sigh.

"It might have been better that you were not," Taylor said. "She was not having one of her better days."

"Yeah. Sarin gas for God's sake."

As they talked, Taylor had been changing his lure from the official ocean one to the recommended mountain stream one. He tried a fly fisherman's toss to get it well away from the pier and saw it drop nicely between waves.

"You said you had something for me?"

Leslie held her wrist unit close to his left hand where his own computer sat. He heard a very soft series of tones as their two computers shared access codes and then synced. "There are those merchant marine types you asked about.

All of them have worked for Nuu shipping lines but are on the beach at the moment."

"Did you include their height, weight, and age?"

Leslie made a face at the ocean. It would not make a dent in her cuteness quotient for the day. "I know Kris Longknife. I know how she knocks her boats around. She damn near retired an entire planet's Navy on disability when she was in Training Command and getting folks up to speed on the fast attack boats. Of course, I gave you that stuff. I don't know what you're up to, boss, but if it includes ships trying to keep up with Kris Longknife, they better be crewed for a fast and wild ride."

"Very good of you, Agent, but please limit your speculation as to what I'm up to, if you will. It's bad enough that I am risking my pension. I do not want you risking yours."

"Understood, boss. By the way, I've put a tracer on most of the folks on that list. I skipped the older types, anyone over forty. Let me know when you lose interest in any of them or decide some old fart like yourself can keep up with my princess."

"Youngster, you are impertinent, and are staying at least one step ahead of your mentor. Yes, I want to know if any of these folks stop by Alex's Tower of Insecurity or the shipyards topside."

"You going to fish tomorrow?"

"I don't know. It all depends on how my other lures and hooks are working."

"I'll drop by when I have something. I might even rent some gear and give you a run for your fish."

"I'm sure they would find you far more attractive than I," Taylor said, with a fatherly smile.

"You bet they would," she said, and headed up the pier without looking back.

Why do you young agents make me feel so old? Taylor thought as he turned back to the ocean. For a long moment, he meditated on it, enjoyed drawing in deep breaths of the ocean air. Certainly, his ancestors must have been people of the coast. Someday, he must check on his roots, but just now, all his investigative skills were fully occupied.

He retrieved his now unbaited hook, added a pair of cubed baits that the box assured him was just the thing to lure half the ocean's fish out of the sea. He checked the area around him to make sure he had it all to himself, then made an even longer cast.

A few minutes later, he became aware he was not alone on the pier.

As he first walked out on the pier, he had taken stock of those on it today. There were the usual collection of fishermen and women. Some plied their rods alone, others in groups that were talkative or silent as was their wont. There were the usual young couples, more interested in each other than the scenery or the fishing whether they had gear or not.

He had spotted Leslie the moment she set foot on the pier, though he had ignored her until she spoke to him. That was no easy thing for an old man to pass up such a lovely sight.

There was nothing lovely about the man now making his way slowly out on the pier. His eyes took the measure of every person on the pier as if they might be secret assassins waiting for his next footstep to strike.

Taylor did not have to task his computer with identifying the man. He remembered him from The Lost Dutchmen's doorway.

For someone undercover, the man had poor spy craft. He had not even bothered to stop and rent fishing tackle.

Taylor took all of this in out of the corner of his eye, and proceeded with his fishing.

Right up to the time that Arlen Cob rested his elbows on the pier's handrail beside Taylor and said, "You catch anything?"

"Not so much as a bite," Taylor answered reeling in his line. He held up the hook. "Empty. The little beggars here must be very good thieves."

The security man refused the bait to talk of thievery. "Good thing, you're not catching anything. It would be an even better idea if you kept you fishing out here on the pier. You know, not dropping your hook in waters where it's not wanted."

Taylor rebaited his line again. This time he put three cubes on the hook. "I doubt if the fish really want me dropping my line in their faces," he said as he whipped the line out, casting it further than before.

"Nice little girl you got running around with you," the security man said.

"Leslie is a special agent of the Wardhaven Bureau of Investigation. She's nobody's little girl." Taylor allowed himself a scowl, but aimed it at the wine dark sea.

"You being on annual leave and her chasing out here to spend her lunch hour with you, people might talk. People might talk even more if two dead bodies were found in the same bed of some cheap hotel, with them in no condition to talk back to them's that talk."

"The Bureau does not take kindly to their agents being killed." This time Taylor aimed his scowl at the man.

His smile was cruel. "Not everyone at the Bureau is as good as you. If a case gets handed off to someone just putting in their time to retirement, it might stay open for a very long time. Especially if, finding the answer might be inconvenient, even embarrassing, to people who don't like to be embarrassed. Do I make myself clear?"

"Are you threatening a Bureau agent?" Taylor said, keeping his temper. Barely.

"Threatening? No, of course not. We're just talking fishing, man. You being on holiday, you wouldn't be recording anything. Me, being on my lunch hour, I left my recorder running. You know what it would show. Just you and me talking about fishing and the weather, and what a nice couple those kids are over there. People would be amazed at your vocabulary, Senior Chief Agent Foile. Amazed. Best if my recording is never called into court, don't you think?"

Foile could tell when he'd been put in check. "Yes," he hissed, like a steam kettle desperate to let off pressure.

"Good. Good that we understand ourselves. Now, I'm going to leave, and you go on fishing. And, oh, by the way, there's some of us that really don't like you. If you hadn't warned that Longknife brat, she'd have charged right out of the elevator and into something she really wasn't ready to play with. No, that kid is definitely not ready to play with the big boys. But you spoiled all that. Shame," Arlen said. He paused, eyeing Taylor to make sure he was following the conversation.

Taylor fumed but said nothing. He'd definitely have something to say. Later.

Through a twisted smile, Arlen went on. "Now some folks down at the office might be holding that against you. Me? I'm not. You just kept missing her, time after time. So, sure, you're hot to get your oar in the water when you get a chance. You shoot off your mouth where it's not wanted. You make a habit of that and it could get you in trouble. You know what I mean?"

"I think I do," Taylor said. Calmly. Oh, so calmly.

"Good, now you enjoy the fishing. I'll be seeing you. Or maybe it would be best if I didn't see you. Ever again."

The man turned and sauntered away. Once in a while he'd look back over his shoulder and chuckle. He really seemed to be enjoying himself.

Taylor reeled in his hook and baited it again. He let his muscles get lost in familiar movement, although he did put the hook through his thumb.

Fortunately, it was only through the outer layer of skin. It was more embarrassing than painful.

Hook cast back into the sea, he let his eyes rove the ocean. With intent, he relaxed his lips and nostrils, forcing them to give up the tension they held.

"You knew this job was dangerous when you took it. Everyone warned you. You're a big boy now. There is no surprise here," he said out loud, trying to believe it.

Oh, yes, there is. The threat against him, his agent, even against Kris Longknife was a bit more than he usually ran into in his Bureau work.

"They warned me that getting too close to one of those damn Longknifes was dangerous," he said to reminded himself, and, what was he close to, three of them. No! Four when you tossed in the father and five if you included Trouble for his proximity to the family. He was way too close to a whole pot full of Longknifes.

"So, Taylor, would now be a good time to fold your cards, toss in your hand and call it quits?"

He thought for a moment. He watched one wave chase another towards the near beach sands.

Suddenly, his line took off running. His mind was so far from the pier that he almost dropped his pole. That was something he hadn't done since he was a boy and his dad took him fishing the first time. He got control before he embarrassed himself for the second time in one noon hour. He let the fish run a bit, then pulled in enough line to make sure the hook was well set, then let him run some more. The fish jumped, trailing the line behind it.

"Hey, that's a big bugger," came from the three old codgers fishing thirty feet further out on the pier. "Ain't seen a core that big for quite a few years."

The three of them gravitated down to him, one offering advice that was usually contradicted by one or both of the others as soon as it was spoken. Taylor did feel that the pressure on the line was letting up and began to reel the fish in.

The core got its second wind and Taylor had to give it more line, but soon enough he was reeling it up to the pier. One of them offered a long-handled net and caught it up. Taylor reeled in the last few feet as the net man hauled it up, hand over hand.

One held the fish while another expertly removed the hook from the fish's mouth.

"She's been hooked a few times," he said. "Just look at her mouth. But this time, you ain't getting away, are you baby?"

"We got to get a picture of this monster," one said, and corralled a pair of the lovers to operate the camera so all four of them, and the fish, could be in it.

Taylor waited until the couple had snapped several pictures, then tossed the fish back over the side.

"Oh," one of the old timers said. "It's a shame you lost your handle on that honey. She'd have fed a family for a week," but the other two seemed to know exactly what happened.

Taylor would gladly take a filleting knife to Arlen Cob. Maybe even Alexander Longknife, but he had no wish to take out his frustrations on some poor fish that just happened to get in his way at the wrong time.

Besides, his wife hated fish, no matter who cleaned them.

Taylor folded up his gear, cleaned it at the washing station, and headed back to where he'd rented it, all the time contemplating the need to warn Leslie and the even stronger need to keep his fingerprints off any alert.

The four retirees were at the rental place. They included one Taylor thought he remembered.

"Albert, can I borrow your phone? Being on vacation, I seem to have left mine on the dresser."

Albert, who'd retired five years ago from the Bureau, couldn't avoid the flick of his eyes that took in the computer at Taylor's wrist, but he was offering his own commlink without batting an eyelash.

Taylor typed out a quick message. I LEFT A FILE RELATING TO OUR LAST CASE IN MY SECURE BRIEFACE. BE CAREFUL RETRIEVING IT, I WOULDN'T WANT YOU SPLASHED WITH ACID.

Taylor handed the commlink back. Albert glanced at the message before he did the unique magic that got messages sent over different net providers and various equipment systems that somehow could never standardize on a single interface.

"The old acid security joke, huh. She a new kid?" Albert asked after reading the old joke.

"Still new enough to benefit from a warning to keep safe," Taylor admitted.

"She the kid that came out to have lunch with you?"

"Yep."

"They get younger every year. Next year, I swear, they'll be recruiting in kindergarten."

Taylor laughed at the old joke and headed for home. With any luck, Leslie would get the message, know what it really meant, and take the caution to heart without it being traced back to Taylor.

He whistled softly to himself as he waited for the bus. One was along as soon as the transit company promised and he was home before the kids got off from school. Today, he'd see if he could still do eighth grade homework. His two upper school kids would, no doubt, turn up their nose at dad's offer of help.

9

Next morning, Taylor actually did do something vacation-like. He took his wife to the Japanese Gardens on a hill above Wardhaven. They walked the quiet grounds, listening to a water wheel and the soft call of birds. Sitting on a cool stone bench, quietly letting a rock garden whisper to them, his wife said.

"You're not really on holiday, are you?"

"I'm here with you," he countered.

"Physically. Today. Yesterday. The day before that. Please don't lie to me, and no, I don't want to know what is actually going on. I've survived twenty-seven years as a Bureau wife. Just don't make me a widow. I deserve the full retirement pension. It may be double of you and half of the pay, but it beats what widows get. You hear me."

"I think I do."

"Good. Be careful."

"I will."

The next day he took her to a movie she'd been wanting to see. The leading character was one his wife swore she was in lust with, almost more than with him. He paid extra to get seats near the center of the theater. That gave them the best view of everything happening around them.

"I love the way you always know when he comes on stage," his wife said. "Some of the new actors these days, they can be on stage a couple of minutes before you know they're there if you aren't looking that way."

'Yes," Taylor agreed. "He always seems to make some sound so you know he's there, a cough, or a misstep."

"He's a pro," his wife agreed.

Which left Taylor wondering what misstep he could catch Alex Longknife in? What would that old and scared man want to sell to the aliens? Computers? Machinery? Most likely, but tracking any particular order among so many would be nearly impossible.

Art work? Food delicacies, wines and other fine spirits? Could orders for those be traced? They would certainly be more limited in their sales. And if there was an order to have them all delivered by a specific date . . . ?

Hmm, that might give us a better call on the fitting out date for those ships overhead.

Taylor made a mental note to himself. The theater done, they walked toward where he'd left their car. "Just a moment, honey, I need to buy something," he said, and ducked into a small store, specializing in off world media, various intoxicants, and, of course, discreet and disposable phones. He paid cash. He always carried a bit of cash for purchases he didn't want traced.

He was an officer of the law, but that didn't mean he had to be dumb.

Using his burner phone, he sent Leslie a text. PLEASE CHECK ORDERS FOR LUXURY ITEMS AND ART. SEE IF THERE IS A PATTERN OF SPECIFIC DELIVERY DATES.

BE CAREFUL. SOME FOLKS ARE PLAYING HARD BALL ON THIS ONE.

His wife was waiting patiently for him when he got back on the street.

"Be careful," was all she said.

"Love, I always am."

10

Next morning, Taylor got the kids off to school, then took himself off to the fishing pier. Again, he had little luck, but he did not change his fishing lure. He kind of liked letting the fish take his bait. The sky was blue with some lovely fluffy clouds floating along with the wind. The water was a clear blue and the air tasted of sun and salt and youth itself.

At lunch, Leslie showed up, two aluminum-wrapped burritos in hand.

"You shouldn't have come. It's dangerous."

"Yeah, So someone told me. Did you have to use that old acid joke? I'm not a probie anymore."

"It got the message out, if not understood," Taylor said, as gruffly as he could. Still he put his rod aside. He did love the burritos created by the food artist at this particular cart.

"It was understood. I'm a big girl and I chose to take it under consideration. I'm considering it still. Now, about the orders for art and high-class consumer goods. There is a pattern. There's a couple of tons of wine, fine cheeses, and delicacies due to be shipped up the beanstalk in two weeks.

Deliveries are spread over three days," she said with a knowing smile.

"On top of that, several art galleries are supposed to deliver pictures, paintings, and sculptures those very same days. Interesting, isn't it? He's also shipping several complete library systems, audio, visual, media, and about half of the books from the Wardhaven public library."

"The technical sections?" Taylor asked.

"Damned if the fool isn't," Leslie said with a scowl.

"He does not pay attention to the news," Taylor said.

"Or at least any that he doesn't think is right," Leslie added. "How much of what passes for news do you believe?"

"I trust the comics. Occasionally the sports section. The rest, well, when it was real paper, it was good to wrap fish in."

"Oh, it's not that bad. The news about Kris Longknife is usually accurate. You can trust her maid for that. She's on Musashi now, awaiting trial. You should watch the one press conference she gave. It was a hoot," the special agent said with a most non-bureau giggle.

"No doubt. No one can accuse her of being a fool," Taylor agreed. "A fool would have lost her head long ago."

Leslie winched. "She may lose her head on Musashi. Quite literally."

"Well, let us not lose our head here. You be careful. Both you and I have been threatened by a certain security type from Alex Longknife's establishment. Keep your eyes open and your back checked."

"I've asked my mother to call me every night," Leslie said. Taylor knew what a sacrifice that was for the agent. "If she can't get ahold of me, she's to call you or Mohomet or Rick. One of you will, no doubt, get the bloodhounds out on my trail."

"No doubt. Now, thanks for the burrito and the news. Get back to work, and again, watch out for our new friends."

"Yes, boss," she said, in a tone no doubt she'd mastered as a teenager for her mother.

He tended to his fishing, but kept a watch on her out of the corner of her eye. She was a delight to watch . . . and she made it off the pier and into the streets of the city without any problems.

Taylor tossed his line back in with four bait cubes. With any luck, the fish would know it for what it was and carefully relieve the hook of its burden without bothering him to reel it in.

Was Alex actually sending a full technical library out to the aliens? What did he expect to get for it? Wine. Cheese. Caviar, no doubt. From what Taylor had picked up about the aliens, they were hardly the type to bother with hors d'oeuvres. No, Alex Longknife was ignoring all that Kris Longknife had reported back about the aliens. He was assuming they were just like him and strutting out there, confident that he, and he alone, understood the situation.

And he'd fall flat on his face, which wasn't so bad, but it would be the greatest catastrophe in human history.

Taylor winced. It would take one of those damn Longknifes to foul up that bad, wouldn't it?

Taylor considered interviewing some of the galleries and purveyors of fine foods, but dropped that line of questioning. They would most likely only know that they had an order and that they were fulfilling it. No leads there.

Again, the agent considered the list of merchant marine officers that Leslie had given him. Yep, they're the most likely source of information. They would have to know something about where they were going and why.

Taylor reeled his hook in. Empty. He rebaited it, putting

six cubes on it, careful to have them loosely affiliated with the hook, and did another cast. He leaned forward, eyes half on the water beneath him, half on his wrist unit as he flipped through the officers.

Every one of them had salient careers with the Star Lines. They'd delivered the goods on time and at a profit. None, Taylor noted, had any experience handling the extraordinary or uncommon. They'd sailed the established trade routes and done the job.

If Alex Longknife thought these men could follow in the footsteps of someone like Kris Longknife, he was a fool.

However, it was very unlikely that anyone that made it to the top of his fortress of insecurity would tell him that.

Taylor looked over the list again, and found nothing new. He rebaited his hook. Eight cubes was all he had, and all the hook would take. Another cast into the ocean void.

Who would I send into the void?

The large freighter would, no doubt, get experience captains and officers. But what about the small tender? Who would take it out? Who would enjoy cloud dancing and, maybe, doing extra scouting?

Taylor went down his list again and found no one with command experience in a cruiser during the war. No one with any experience in the little stuff.

My list is too short.

Taylor reeled in his hook, collected his gear and headed to the wash area. Clean and done, he returned it to the rental. None of the retirees there today were from the bureau. He put five bucks into the tip bucket and headed for the bus stop.

Half his mind was on where he might find the missing skipper, someone to command the tender. The other half of his mind, was, as normal, checking out his own situation.

There were the usual joggers and skaters. Business men and women went from their last meeting to their next one. Here and there, a couple strolled along, intent on each other.

A limo pulled up to the stop light.

The bus he wanted turned onto the street. Taylor turned to watch it as it headed toward him.

Suddenly, a couple that he'd have sworn were too interested in each other to bother anyone stepped up to him. The door in the limo opened and he was shoved into it.

He opened his mouth to scream, but a small prick at his neck did something and the day turned dark before he could get a sound out.

11

Taylor came aware of his surroundings slowly. Before opening his eyes, he took stock of matters and found them grave.

He was seated in a comfortable chair. His hands were cuffed in his lap. He could also feel restraints at his ankles. In all likelihood, the two were chained together.

His first glace upon opening his eyes verified that. He kept his chin resting on his chest and surveyed his surroundings through slit eyelids.

The room looked comfortable, in an expensive way. The rug was white, the chair and sofa he could see were white leather. The walls were a sterile white as well.

If they beat me up, the blood will sure make a mess of the decor.

Taylor didn't find his joke funny.

Arlen Cob sauntered into the room. "Ah, sleeping beauty has awoken. I feared I'd have to give you the required kiss."

"It only works if true love is behind it," Taylor said, dryly. "But I would trouble you for a drink. Water, please."

"I think that can be arranged," and Arlen left the room.

A moment later he returned with an icy glass of water and a straw. He brought the straw to Taylor's lips and the agent sucked up half the glass in one gulp.

"Yeah, I'm told that stuff dries you out," he said. "There's more cool stuff where that came from."

"So, you don't intend for me to die of thirst. Starve?"

"We intend to return you to your life, untouched by angry human hands, right about the time your leave runs out."

"How nice, and, no doubt, after the ships have sailed."

The security man's smile was pure evil. "I don't know nothing about no ships."

Taylor looked around the room. "Comfortable place you got here."

"We like to think it is. In time, I think you'll find it that way. We can provide all kinds of amenities, once you understand that you aren't going anywhere. Why, I've even been given a cash allotment to give you so you can join in our poker game. We really want you to think of this as a holiday."

"And not a kidnaping?"

"Oh, you strike me to the quick," Arlen said, raising his free fist to his heart. "Such a strong word for folks that just want you to enjoy your holiday and not waste it poking your nose where it don't belong."

"Into what *you* don't want me to know."

"Six one way, half a dozen the other," the security man said. "Just so long as you understand that you are not leaving here for the next two, three weeks, we'll get along fine."

"And if I refuse your hospitality?"

"That would be a major mistake, Agent. A major mistake. We can do this the easy way, and you can join our poker game, swim in our pool. Share the hot tub with some truly lovely gals that don't own a swim suit among them. Maybe share other stuff they got that you wouldn't believe," he said with a friendly leer.

All the friendly was gone in a blink. "Or we can do this the hard way. I got more of that shit we used on you. We can keep you out for a long, long time. 'Course, I understand that it ain't healthy for a man of your age to spend a couple of weeks in bed. It could lead to embolisms and other messy stuff. It's your call. Choose wisely."

And with that, Arlen left the room, leaving Taylor to contemplate his sins: past, present and future.

Alone, Taylor tested the boundaries of his imprisonment. The cuffs on his hands were linked to his ankles with a chain that let him move a bit, but not enough to reach his pants pockets, assuming they hadn't been emptied, and assuming he was carrying anything useful.

His leggings were not only chained to his cuffs, but had chains going to each leg of the chair. His feet couldn't move more than a centimeter or two to the right or left.

He managed to struggle to his feet. He had to stand stooped over; the chain to his legs was not long enough to stand fully upright. He tried to shuffle forward.

The chair would not move. Whether it was just too heavy or somehow secured to the floor, it wasn't going anywhere, nor was he with it.

He sat back down. As much as he hated to admit that the security flake was right about anything, Taylor could already feel his blood pooling towards his feet. Sitting, hour after hour, was not going to go well.

So, old boy, what do you do? Have them deal you in, or what?

Taylor hated the question. He hated the answer even more.

If he stayed here in the chair, the situation would remain static. If he played along, he might get an opening. Criminals always made mistakes. If he played their game, he might get an opening.

But keep your pants on, old friend. No doubt, they'll have cameras around to capture anything worthy of blackmail.

Assuming they didn't digitize him into a compromising position anyway.

From somewhere, the heavenly smell of steaks on a grill wafted through the room, and Taylor found it had been a long time since breakfast.

It was thirty minutes before Arlen returned. "What's it going to be? Steaks fresh from the grill or a bottle of sugar water jabbed into your arm?"

Taylor scowled. "I will escape."

"I fully expect you to try. You won't," had finality in it.

Taylor found himself freed from his chair and allowed to shuffle to the next room. A spacious kitchen and dining room had a table that clearly had been the center of a poker game only a few minutes before. The three men now lounging around it had the distinct air of alertness and power. They also looked like they were very comfortable with the automatics that hung ready in their shoulder holsters.

One end of the room faced an expansive patio and pool. Through large French doors, a fifth man brought in large platter with a huge steak, a baked potato slathered in butter, and an ear of corn. With a cautious eye, the armed cook set the steak before Taylor.

The agent eyed it hungrily. "Do I eat it with my hands, guys?" Taylor asked.

The hard cases enjoyed a laugh and Arlen produced a steak knife with a serrated edge but a well-rounded end. "You aren't getting away from us," his kidnaper said.

They waited for him to get fully involved with his steak, there was just enough play in the wrist restraints for him to eat if he bowed his head to meet the fork, before they went outside one by one to return with their own platters. The table chatter was focused on the upcoming hockey championship. Taylor followed the sports pages enough to make a few comments on the chances the Accomack Fliers would have against the Wicomico White Lightnings.

The book said it was a good idea to help your kidnappers see you were a human being like them. Arlen might be saying he didn't intend Taylor any harm, but the agent hadn't heard that from the rest.

Besides, in a situation like this, things were always subject to change.

The steaks were hardly eaten when the girls arrived. What little they wore didn't stay on after a dip in the pool or the hot tub. The kidnappers enjoyed their very available feminine gifts. Taylor had to work hard to keep his pants on, not that that kept each of the girls from trying her hand at getting him into the fun.

"You know you want me," each of them would purr, taking him firmly in hand.

"Thank you, but I think I'll pass," Taylor said, time after time. No doubt they would produce a film of him fully involved in the orgy, but he wanted to be able to face his wife and say, "That is a fake. I didn't do anything of the sort."

He also wanted to pass a Bureau of Investigation polygraph test.

While he was trying not to gawk at the live porn action around him, he studied what he could see out the window. There were hills in his view. His best guess was that he was in a house deep in the foothills to the west of Wardhaven. He doubted they were all the way to the mountains.

With any luck, the recording of this, with him no doubt naked and *flagrante*, would also have some of the scenery. His agents would be able to locate the house from that.

Assuming he survived long enough for them to attempt black mail, or whatever Alex Longknife intended to do to cover up this bit of kidnaping.

Through the carrying on, Taylor kept his eye out for an escape, but while a lot came up, an escape wasn't one of them. All through it, one of the guards was seated a meter or so from him. Well out of reach for a lunge, something that would be worthless, anyway, in his shackled condition. His guards never got close enough for him to make a grab for their gun.

"Isn't it the pits when the bad guys hire people good at what they do?" Arlen said with a smirk when it was his turn to keep watch.

"Yeah, the boys like to play, and I make sure they get a good chance at it, but no, none of them is going to slack on the job. We know what needs doing, and we do it. For example, note your computer and burner phone," he said with a wave of his hand to the counter where the contents of Taylor's pockets lay spread out.

"We took the battery out of your computer and the chip and battery out of your phone. Did it as soon as you were out cold in the car. No locator is going to find you."

Arlen walked over to the counter and picked up the batteries. "We won't be needing these, will we?" he said, and dropped them into a glass of water.

Correction, glass of acid. The contents of the glass bubbled and the batteries dissolved. Then the kidnapper added the phone chip. "There, you can quit looking at your gear. Even if you managed to hop your way over here, there's be nothing you could do to make any of this junk work. You're screwed, even if you won't enjoy the entertainment we're offering you."

"I will escape," Taylor said, doing his best to make it sound ominous, though he still had no idea how he might pull it off.

"In your dreams, boyo. In your dreams," Arlen said, his back to Taylor as his hands wondered through the agent's pocket contents.

"My, now what is this?" the kidnaper said, raising a sphere to eye level.

"That's a marble my father gave me. I keep it as a kind of good luck piece," Taylor said, lying through his teeth. It was the sphere Trouble's Tech mage had given him. What it did, he still had no idea, but he wasn't about to tell this bunch of criminals that.

"You, a hard-headed type, believe in magic? I think not."

"My father died two years ago," Taylor said, finding no problem telling this painful truth. "It reminds me of him. I roll it around in my hand when I have a tough call to make and ask myself, 'What would dad do'?"

"What do you know? Someone who cares about his old man. Me, I would have spat on his grave, but his fourth wife cremated him and kept the ashes on her mantelpiece. She's got a collection there, now. Four husbands. She would have hired me some girls for this, if I'd made her an offer."

Taylor wondered how this bit of self-revelation would end up. Not the rambling talk, but the fate of the sphere.

Arlen held it up to the light. "It's got all kinds of colors in it," he muttered, then he put it in his own pocket.

"Ask me for it nice when we let you go and I may give it back to you."

"You really want to add theft to kidnaping?" Taylor asked.

That got him a nasty face, but the head honcho pulled the sphere from his pocket and, carefully approaching Taylor from behind, slipped it into his left pants pocket. "There, you happy?"

"Thank you," Taylor said.

"You're welcome."

The sun was well down before the girls were sent packing. They made a final attempt on Taylor but he managed to keep as much of his virtue intact as conditions allowed. Arlen sent them on their way with a large bonus and then had his four henchmen see that Taylor was put to bed and shackled to it most securely.

One man was ordered to the comfortable chair Taylor had awoken in. "We'll trade off every two hours. Don't worry, Boyo, you won't get lonesome."

With not much to do, and little chance to do it, Taylor decided to let himself sleep. They might kill him, but trussed up like he was, he wouldn't be able to stop them. He'd learned as a soldier to get his sleep when he could. No use being tired when the chance came.

To Taylor's surprise, he fell asleep rather quickly.

12

He came awake to someone gently shoving his foot back and forth.

"Wakey wakey, boss," came in Leslie's delightful voice.

"Aren't you up past your bedtime?" Taylor said, fully awake and alert to not only his subordinate laughing at his question, but a large number of uniformed, armored, and armed men and women moving about the room. One produced a pair of cutters and soon Taylor was free to sit up in bed.

"We're hunting for the key to the cuffs and shackles," Leslie said.

"What took you so long?" he grumbled, unable to think of anything better to fill the silent void.

"Well, we took a wrong turn twice, but other than that, I think we did rather well."

"What's it been, twelve hours since they snatched me?"

"Your wife called me when you didn't make it home to help the kids with their homework. Boss, do you really think someone as old as you can keep up with the kids today?"

"No, but I like to think I can. And then what happened?"

"Your boss declared you missing when I explained what we'd been up to."

"I would have thought she'd say good riddance."

"You wrong her greatly, boss, and be careful. She's in the next room. Anyway, it was easier than we expected. You know when you asked me to put a trace on those Merchant Marine skippers?"

"Yes."

"Well, I put a trace on you, too, then double checked it when you pulled that acid briefcase joke on me. Good thing I did. We knew your computer, and I did a check on your burn phone, but we found a third trace on you. Quiet little thing, something that showed up but we couldn't do an ID on. Still, where you went, it went, so we tagged it into our tracker. You have any idea what it was? Because the other two went dead after you left the fishing pier. That one just kept on whispering 'Here I am. Come get me!'"

"I'll tell you about it later," Taylor said, managing to wiggle himself out of bed while his hands were still cuffed and his feet still shackled. Not having them chained together was almost wonderful.

"Here's the key," Rick Sanchez said, coming in the room. "Boss, did you really get your ass into an orgy?"

"No," Taylor said firmly, and maybe a bit primly.

"You know he didn't Rick, we had him under surveillance before the entertainment arrived," Leslie said, just as primly.

"Well, there's a video running out there that shows him dipping his wick with the best of these thugs," Rick said. "I'm thinking of keeping a copy to keep me warm in my long bachelorhood.

"Destroy it." Taylor said.

"Can't," Rick shot back. "The big boss says it's evidence. We'll match our video against theirs and call it conspiracy to blackmail."

Taylor shrugged. "The bigger book we can throw at them, the better. How soon can I get Arlen in an interrogation room?"

"Ah, boss," Leslie said, "you're up to your neck in this case. You can't do the investigation."

"This is not a case. It will never see a judge," Taylor said. "It's too hot to go that route. It will be handled otherwise, for better or worse. Now, let's get downtown and see how well Mr. Arlen Cob can sing."

13

The surroundings were familiar and drab. A table. Some chairs. A prisoner in cuffs. This prisoner was cool. Arlen had been cool from the moment Taylor first saw him in the doorway of the Lost Dutchmen.

How do I break that ice?

Taylor nodded to his boss and subordinates, took the formal paper that his boss handed him, and went to beard the cool Mr. Cob.

In the interrogation room, Taylor crossed to the table and sat down facing Cob.

"We'll make this short and sweet," Cob said calmly. "I want my lawyer. He'll be here in ten minutes, then we'll begin a lawsuit that will have the bureau giving me its budget for the next five years. Other than this, I ain't saying a word."

"Terrorists don't get lawyers," Taylor said just as calmly.

"You can accuse me of kidnaping you. Nothing else. And that will never go to court."

Was there a hint of worry there?

Taylor pressed on. "We'll ignore the other charges against you for now. I don't hold a grudge. But you, me boyo," Taylor had to admit he liked the slight involuntary flinch he got from Cob at turning that familiarity around, "are charged with aiding and abetting a terrorist. Under the law, terrorists and their allies don't get lawyers."

"There's no such law!" came in an explosion from Cob.

"Oh, but my bureau lawyers tell me there is. An old, one might even call it ancient, law, folded into the Society of Humanity's judicial code from long ago, and, as it seems, left in our legal code from our days in that bygone society. Yep, boyo, you're a terrorist and will be tried under those codes."

Cob was at a loss for words. His lips moved, but nothing came out. Finally, he took a deep breath. "I am no terrorist. I'm not aiding and abetting any terrorist. I don't know where you dreamed that up, but you've got nothing like that on me. Sooner or later, you'll have to answer my employer, and then," his confident smirk came back, "I'll own your ass."

"On the contrary. You and your employer are involved in aiding and abetting terrorists. To wit, delivering equipment and technology under the proscribed articles listed for foreign sale to alien terrorists bent on the destruction of all humanity," Taylor kept his voice as matter of fact as twenty years of work at the law allowed him. He tasted the sound of his voice and found it good.

Cob had the smarts to blink several times after the charge was given him. Then he shook his head.

"I don't know nothing about no shipment of anything to aliens, or anybody else," came out calm, but the "I swear to God," showed he was taking the heat to heart.

"You were told to hold me for two, maybe three weeks. Strange that. Over the next two weeks, a large shipment of technical information, a library to keep it in, and examples of quite a lot of restricted gear and machinery was due to be shipped up to the Nuu Yards. In two weeks' time, a pair of huge ships fitting out there were also due to be completed. Coincidence? I doubt it."

Taylor paused to let that sink into Cob's thick skull.

"Those ships during construction were specifically modified from what you'd expect for conventional trade among human planets to specific conditions suitable only for going out to make contact with the space aliens Kris Longknife encountered in her circumnavigation of the galaxy. With the cargo arranged for them and the technological information in them, those huge alien mother ships could beat a quick trail to our door. You've seen the pictures of what those monster ships look like, haven't you?"

"Yeah, I saw it. Couldn't miss if for the couple of days it was on the news." Cob was actually showing signs of being thoughtful. "Ugly things. I remember when it was just six battleships threatening to blow Wardhaven back to the Stone Age."

The kidnapper's eyes wandered off to the left wall of the interrogation room. "People were pretty pissed about that. That Kris Longknife was the toast of the town for a whole week."

"It did wonders for her dad's re-election, didn't it?"

"Yeah. Bunch of sheep," Cob snapped. Then seemed to think better of it. "But this is still a political matter. It's gonna be settled by the Longknifes, not by sending me to jail."

"You sure of that? Even if we take it that you were just an uninformed pawn, you're still up for kidnaping an agent of the Bureau of Investigations in furtherance of a conspiracy to provide critical secrets to the most God-awful terrorists we've ever seen. Remember those pictures of the mother ship? Huge. Imagine the mob of soldiers they've got."

The prisoner gulped. Hard.

"But, you didn't know. Still, you won't be seeing a conventional court. You'll be sentenced, probably for life. You hear any stories about our prison on HellFrozeOver? I understand they use the prisoners for genetic experiments. Stuff too deadly or dangerous to risk anywhere closer to Wardhaven."

Cob's mouth opened, but nothing came out.

Taylor gauged the emotions running riot on his prisoner's face. Denial didn't get much play time. No, most of it was raging terror, descending in a vicious cycle from bad to worse.

It had been a long time since there had been any problem with terrorists. Still, every couple of years there would be a spat of movies on the topic. Each generation seemed to make the deeds of the terrorists more despicable . . . and the response of society more brutal and horrendous.

Taylor wondered which movies were playing in Cob's mind.

"What can I tell you?" came out as little more than a whisper as the man's stare fixed on the table.

Cob was broken.

"I want to know about ship captains. Merchant ship officers. Have you been involved in tracking any of them? Do you know anyone who has?" Taylor shot his words hard and fast, machine gun fashion.

Cob seemed to reel back in his seat. He took two deep breaths before saying a word.

"Me, no, *I* got *you*," came out more as spit than words.

"Who has the merchant marine officers?" Taylor knew

he was fishing in thin air, still he cast his hook, sure there was a bigger fish out there somewhere.

"Kittikon. He got asked to check out some merchant skippers for the old man. He thought it was scut work. Nothing to it, except for one. 'Crazy shit coming out of the top floors,' he told me over a beer, two, no, three weeks ago. They had him chasing down a skipper for the Star Line that had never sailed a mile in a freighter. He thought maybe the old man was going senile. The gal was a commander in the Navy. A real hot rodder in her destroyer. That mean anything to you?" was more a plea than a question.

"And where might I find this Kittikon?" Taylor asked.

"I don't know. I haven't seen him much around the shop lately. But then, you were keeping me kind of busy. You got a lot of friends in high places."

"And you reported all my comings and goings."

"Yep, every one of them. Well, all but that dame you met at the Galleria. Who was she?"

"As you're aware, I ask the questions, you answer them," Taylor said, hardly willing to tell this man that he knew no more about this technical whizz than he did. "I believe you may have been of some help, Mr. Cob. I'll see that something to eat is brought into you."

"A steak with all the trimmings?" he said, slipping back into the something of the wise ass he'd been earlier.

"Not on the bureau's budget."

"Thanks for nothing."

"It will be better than jail fare, I assure you," Taylor said, and headed next door to consult with his boss and Leslie.

The young agent was already using her wrist unit to call up Mr. Kittikon.

"Employed by Nuu Security for the last ten years. He seems to have gone up the organization with more than the usual speed. No criminal involvement. Not so much as a traffic ticket in our database," Leslie reported.

"Can we track him?" the boss asked.

"No ma'am," Leslie replied. "I tried as soon as Cob here spit out his name. Nuu agents usually stay on the grid, but this guy has been off it for, oh, the last three weeks."

"So, this problem has been developing for the last three weeks," Taylor said. "Since before Kris Longknife paid her visit to us. She was right, this project has been underway for at least a month. Likely from the time they changed the design of those two ships in the Nuu Yard," Taylor said.

"So, we need to track someone off the grid," the boss said. She gnawed her lower lip for a long moment, then made her call. "Agent Chu, you are authorized to access the Prometheus database. I will have a letter added to your file from me authorizing this as soon as I can get back to my desk. Get started on it now."

Both Taylor's and Leslie's eyebrows shot up. Prometheus was a project left over from the long ago Iteeche War. It took in all the take from every camera on Wardhaven, both private and public, and collected it into one huge database. Officially, no one had access to it. Taylor had not even dared to ask to access it to track Kris Longknife, but had made due with the usual piecemeal data pulls that the authorities regularly used.

Prometheus was so off limits that officially, it didn't exist. Still, parliament regularly granted the small sums needed to increase the project's storage servers the tiny staff of technicians needed to handle the new feeds that they kept adding to the project.

It was too powerful for anyone to use, but also too powerful for those in power to give up.

Taylor's boss would be in very hot water when it was

found she'd authorized its use. Prometheus, being moribund, had no procedures for authorizing access. No one has authority, not even the prime minister, to grant access to Prometheus.

No doubt, that topic would come up later.

14

Two hours later, Taylor was wondering what all the excitement was about Prometheus. It didn't appear to be worth a damn.

Of course, part of the problem was that they were accessing data in the vicinity of the Longknife Tower. Taylor had concluded that the tower would be the perfect place to pick up the trail of Security Specialist Kittikon.

He was very wrong.

In the recent past, while in hot pursuit of Kris Longknife, Taylor had gained some personal experience with the level of security at Longknife Tower. He had not been impressed.

Now, the agent began to wonder if that atrociously poor quality was an intended feature rather than a byproduct of poor management or tightfisted folly.

The cameras feeding Prometheus went down time and time again, usually during the height of the business day.

Leslie had several recent photos of Security Specialist Kittikon. After an hour of running it through the database, going back over everyone recorded entering the tower for the last six weeks, they did not have a single hit on him.

"Maybe if we back our search away from the tower's cameras. Get into territory where the cameras don't go up and down like ping pong balls," Leslie suggested.

So, they backed the search out. That gave them a lot more data to run through, both because it covered a lot more territory, and because it didn't have gaping holes in the coverage

It was late at night, and they'd only done a week, when Taylor insisted they go home. "The machine will have something to tell us tomorrow morning and that will be soon enough."

He got Leslie to leave by asking her for a ride home.

His kids were delighted to see him. His wife let them fawn over him for a long hour, even condescended to play a board game with them, then showed them off to bed and led him by the hand to their bed.

"You were missed," she whispered, then showed him why he hadn't taken all that much interest in the orgy by the pool. When he came up for air, she cuddled close.

"Don't you ever terrify me like that again."

"I was never in any danger, love."

"Don't lie to me."

"I wasn't, really. They intended to keep me out of circulation for two or three weeks, then turn me loose with the threat of releasing some very embarrassing pictures if I complained."

"How were they going to get the pictures?"

"You can do a lot with computers these days. Leslie told me the bureau had me on camera the entire time they had me. I was a good boy."

"No doubt you were," she said, and pulled him close. "You're my good boy, remember that."

"With moments like these, how could I not?" he said, and held her close until she began to breathe softly in sleep.

Only then did he shudder.

If he'd been held the entire two weeks, he had no idea how it might have ended. Could he have stayed good? If he had, would they have been happy to create their blackmail video or would someone have decided that a dead agent was worth the risk?

For the millionth time, he thanked any God listening that he had a team as good as his and a boss so understanding.

Somehow, he fell asleep.

Next morning, it was the sound of his boys arguing with his daughter that woke him. She was for a nutritious breakfast. They were for something less so. She won before he managed to make it downstairs. She was rather proud of herself that she had fixed breakfast for the four of them.

"You'll serve mom later, won't you Dad?"

"Of course, dear."

They seemed to linger at the door until he sent them on their way with a series of hugs and promises to be there when they got home, then he prepared toast and applesauce for his slumbering wife.

Or not so slumbering. She was waiting for him as he brought the tray upstairs. Can a wife sexually assault her husband?

Is it assault if he is a willing participant?

It didn't matter who jumped whose bones. They leapt at the same moment.

He was late getting back to the office.

Security Specialist Kittikon was still eluding the mighty Prometheus.

"We've covered the area around the tower. We've covered

several of Alex Longknife's other residences. We've gone over all the major and most of the minor offices of the Star Lines," Leslie said. "Kittikon has not showed up at any of them in the last eight weeks."

"When did you come in this morning?" Taylor asked.

"Early," was the most specific any of his team would confess to.

Taylor pulled up a chair and stared out the window for a long minute. Maybe two. Well, at least five.

"Clearly," he said slowly, "this Kittikon fellow does not want to be recognized. Kris Longknife was not recognized when she crossed the space station to the elevator, or aboard it either, now was she?"

"Disguise," Leslie said.

"That would be kind of admitting that you were up to no good," Rick said.

"Clearly, he is not," Mahomet concluded.

"So, what do we have to go on?" Taylor asked.

"His height," Rick said. "We could make some allowance for elevator shoes or a slouch."

"And run it all again," Leslie said, despair for the length of time clearly in her voice.

"But we're not just after him, now, are we?" Taylor said, posing the question. "He had to be bringing in a skipper for that tender."

"Two people," Leslie said, slowly.

"Should we search for recent Navy destroyer captains now on the beach?" Rick asked.

"It would not do us any good," Mahomet pointed out, "If Kittikon is in full disguise, so would he or she be?"

"So, we hunt for two men. Or a man and a woman. No, two people?" Leslie said.

Taylor smiled as his protégé caught on. "And we follow

them out until they go into a rest room and come out different."

"This is going to take a lot of computer power," Leslie said.

"I'll go talk to the boss."

The boss did her best, but Taylor did better. He used his new-found in with a senior member of parliament to get access to the Ministry of Defense's spare computers as well.

Still, it took a whole lot more time than they had.

A week later, Leslie bounced out of her chair and began doing a rather cute victory dance. "Yes! Yes! I have her!"

"Her? I thought we were after a him?" Rick asked.

"Yes, but he's a her at the moment."

"Explain," Taylor said.

"Here we have two well-dressed matrons entering a lady's room at a shopping emporium about a mile from Longknife Tower. They never leave that room, not for the six hours until closing. No exit."

The team was gathering around to watch the action on the wall screen. Even the boss seemed to have been called in.

"However, here we have two rather attractive young women leaving the facility, some fifteen minutes later. They never entered it. The computer spotted this discrepancy. I had it check all the way back and forward through the day, then follow the matrons back to the tower, or as close as we could get to it before the cameras puked out on us. They were in a taxi. One of the better ones. They left here in a town car. Again, one of the better ones."

"Is that Kittikon?" the boss asked.

"Allowing for the minor discrepancy in gender, the computer gives us a 39.58% chance it's Kittikon. That's too low for us to normally get a hit on the search routine, but I lowered the threshold. The other 'woman' is as much a mystery. She doesn't cause a hit in any of our searches. However, when I lowered the probability to 35%, I got 56 potential hits. What's interesting is that one of them is a former destroyer skipper."

"Former?" the boss asked.

"Commander Megan Zloben was relieved of her command by her superior for the rather general reason of 'loss of confidence.' What does that mean, boss?"

Taylor made a face. "It means her superior no longer had confidence in her ability to command the ship."

"That sounds rather vague," Leslie said. "And not all that fair."

"I have the file here," Rick said. "It says she failed to properly mentor her subordinates."

"Gosh, boss," Leslie said, eyes way too wide, "are you getting credit for making us a great team?"

"Something like that," his boss said. "It appears that this commander knows how to drive a ship, but not how to build a crew."

"And she's on the beach," Taylor said.

"And a certain Alex Longknife is more interested in her driving a ship whether or not she drives her crew to drink."

"He's likely paying top dollar," Mahomet pointed out. "They can put up with a bit of Captain Bligh."

"So, where is she?" Taylor's boss asked.

"The computer is tracking the two of them. Their town car passed through several areas not under surveillance. When we next see it, it's taking on a new fare," Leslie reported. "I've got it working, ma'am."

"You keep it working. Taylor, you go home. This was supposed to be your vacation time, remember?"

"My wife won't let me forget."

It was two days later that they finally tracked them to a small villa down the coast.

15

Despite the massive array of force that followed them to the villa, Taylor persuaded his boss into letting him just walk up and knock on the door. She did assure that two vanloads of select SWAT teams were just a short run away.

Taylor's knocked, but no one answered.

"Mr. Kittikon, Commander Zloben, I know you're in there," Taylor shouted.

No one still answered.

"I'm not going away. You may open the door, or I will open it, but either way, it is time we meet."

The security specialist opened the door a crack. He was bare chested and in his undershorts. Maybe gym shorts.

"I'm here alone."

"Then you won't mind me coming in to talk to you."

"As a matter of fact, I do mind, and you may not come in."

"Then I will share with you the search warrant I have to go over these premises."

"You have no reason to get a search warrant."

"Yes. Your file shows you have a law degree. However, I know a judge who lost her youngest daughter on the *Furious* under Kris Longknife's command. She has a most intense interest in seeing that her daughter did not die in vain."

The door opened. Taylor was led into a wide sitting room. Commander Zloben was reclined on a leather couch in a most revealing tank top and even more revealing bikini underwear.

"Good morning, Commander," Taylor said, taking a seat in a matching leather chair across from her.

"And you are?" she said, raising an eyebrow, but not coming to her feet.

"I am Senior Chief Agent in Charge Taylor Foile. I have been on your trail for some time. I am glad to make your acquaintance."

"I don't know why." she said, waving Kittikon over. He settled beside her and she proceeded to stroke him in a most salacious manner.

Taylor addressed himself to the security specialist. "The ships are fitting out. When is Commander Zloben taking command of the tender?"

"You seem to know a lot more about this than I do. Why don't you tell me?" he said, responding to her stoking by brushing aside the wisp of her top to begin stroking her erect nipple.

So, Taylor told the two of them the story he had pieced together. Several furtive and alarmed glances interrupted their affectation of foreplay to confirm Taylor's suspicions.

He had guessed right.

"So, why don't you tell me where the fleet is going?" Taylor concluded. "I suppose we could hold the two

Longknife freighters and the tender in port, but I suspect that those three ships are not the entirety of the foolishness."

The commander pulled down the security man's shorts and began fondling him in full view of the agent.

"Why should I tell you anything?" she said.

"Because, if these aliens run true to form, you and your crew will be dead in a couple of weeks if you don't cooperate with us."

The commander actually interrupted her sex play to eye Taylor. "What makes you think that? You haven't told me anything I don't already know. I did watch the reports that came back with that Kris Longknife girl. But as for these aliens killing me, you have not thought this through. No, not at all," she said, and returned her attention to her sex partner.

"What do you think I've missed?" Taylor said.

She didn't even look back at him, but toyed like a cat with what was in front of her.

"I command a fast tender. I refuel the ships when they need it, but that also means I can refuel myself any time I want to. I've got almost unlimited range," she said, and demonstrated it by roving her fingernails, claw like, over Kittikon's thighs and chest and all in between.

"As I see it, when they meet up with the aliens, I hang well back. If things go well, I'm in on the ground floor of a huge profit maker. If it goes sour, well, I run," she said, and ran her fingers up Kittikon's chest, and back down.

"After all, someone has to bring the word back, and I figure I can run just as fast as that Longknife brat."

"And the aliens will follow you back."

"Did they follow her back?" the commander asked, and

applied herself to her toy, who responded with a delighted moan. "Let's say, you're right. The aliens find out where we are from the freighter's nav gear. I still have a ship. I've got several cute boys and girls in its crew. I know some really wonderful desert planets that aren't on anyone's charts. I set myself up fine. Maybe I make a few trips out to get what we need. Maybe I sell passenger slots on my ship to folks that want to run too. I really don't see a down side, mister-whoever-you-are. Now," she said, slithering out of her bottom, "you interrupted a nice roll in the hay. If you want, you can stay and watch, but, please, be quiet."

Taylor had interrogated a lot of criminals in his time. He'd learned to use silence as a scalpel to cut through resistance and get to the cancerous tumor of crime. Never had he been at a loss for words.

The total self-absorption and self-interest of this former Navy commander lolling in front of him left him speechless.

He let himself out. Behind him, someone groaned. Someone else laughed.

"Did what we think just happened actually happen?" came from Leslie in his earbud.

"It most certainly did," Taylor whispered, as he made his way toward the Bureau's surveillance van. "You can send the SWAT folks home, unless they want to make it an orgy."

"They're taking a vote on that," Leslie said.

Taylor adjusted himself before he entered the van. Yes, he was intent on the mission, but he had eyes, and they were connected to a male brain.

"So, what do we do?" his boss asked.

"Rick, Leslie, monitor all communications from that house," Taylor ordered.

"I would think they'd be otherwise involved," Rick said.

"We got a message coming out," Leslie said.

"As I expected, the display was to discomfort me," Taylor said. "No doubt, it ended the moment I left the building."

"Damn," Leslie said."

"Damn for what?" Taylor said.

"For something interruptus," Leslie said, "and for the message. It was just a squirt of something in code. And it was addressed to a number that isn't in our database."

"The Bureau has every net number on the planet," the boss said.

"Not this one," Leslie countered.

"It must be nice to have produced and sold our planet's communications security system," Taylor said, dryly. "No doubt there are several numbers not in our database."

"I'm tracking that number," Leslie said. "It just made a call to another one. It shot the same message out. Oh, and that number also isn't one we know about. It's going to another number. This may take a while."

"And, no doubt, the message is flashing faster than we are tracking it. It will get somewhere well before we follow it," Taylor said.

"No doubt," his boss said. "Any idea what it says?"

"If it says anything other than, 'we've been found out,' you may have my pension," Taylor said.

"I think your pension is safe," she said. "So, what happens now?"

"I suspect that a well-laid plan will get sped up," Taylor said. "Rick, check out the orders that were placed for cargo. How much has been delivered?"

"About half so far," he reported. "Oh, what don't you know? They've just begun to speed up the scheduled deliveries. They're also canceling anything that can't be delivered by noon tomorrow."

"That was fast," his boss said.

"I suspect that our attention has not gone unnoticed," Taylor said. "I would bet that when we accessed Prometheus, a flag went up in Longknife Tower. No doubt, this need for speed was not totally unexpected."

"They're moving," came from the driver of the van. Taylor stuck his head out of the back and got a view of the commander and Kittikon, now dressed in shirts and slacks, jumping into the car in the driveway. In a moment, it gunned into the street and took off.

"Shall we follow them?"

His boss tossed the question to Taylor with a raised eyebrow.

"I suspect they're headed for the beanstalk and from there to the Nuu Yards. Leslie, check all those merchant marine officers you identified. How many of them are on the move?"

"About two dozen. No, twenty-seven."

"That's an odd number," Mahomet said.

Taylor frowned in thought, but his boss gave voice to the problem first. "A lot of them moving, but none of them compromised. How do we get someone to talk to us?"

"Usually, something comes up," Taylor said. "They are the bad guys."

"But these bad guys are really good," Leslie said with a frown on her usually optimistic young face.

Taylor's commlink buzzed. He tapped it.

"Agent Foile," Member of Parliament Longknife said.

"Here, sir."

"I just got a call from Annie Smedenhoff. It seems her boyfriend has just been ordered up the beanstalk to join the crew of the *Pride of the Free Market*. He was told something about the intended navigator being on a ship coming in, but they want to sail now. Annie's in a panic. She told him what she thinks the *Prides* are up to, and he's not at all interested in going, but it seems to me that we need someone on one of those ships."

"We most certainly do, sir," Taylor said, smiling at Leslie. She grinned back, made a fist and punched air. "When does he have to be headed up?" the special agent asked.

"He's been told he has four hours to pack."

"Tell him, and Annie, to take all of the four hours. I'll see what I can do about arranging something."

"You do that. I've got to get going on something else. The whole damn fleet's out on maneuvers and there aren't many available to tail those ships."

"We don't really want to be obvious on their tail, sir."

"I've watched enough TV to know that, Agent. You do what you can do. I'll do what I have to," and he rang off.

Taylor found himself staring at the roof of the surveillance van. The others stayed silent as he thought.

Then he tapped his commlink. He called a number he had only used twice.

A woman's voice answered him. "You have problems, I see."

"If you are following me, then you know I need to have someone get a message off a starship before it jumps out of the system, but no one must know it has been sent."

"I think I have something at hand. Meet me at the Galleria. I'll be waiting for you outside."

Things must be critical. The woman blew her cover by being there, pacing back and forth, as they rolled up. She jumped in the van and ordered. "Head for the space elevator station."

The van moved quickly through traffic.

"I have a ring," the tech magician said without preamble. "It will remember what it types. It can burst transmit that memory with a simple command. Three twists around the finger causes it to send."

"So, how do we get it to the navigator?" Taylor's boss mused.

"Rick and I could be a couple," Leslie said, "with me headed up the beanstalk. We could do a brush-by of the guy."

Taylor shook his head. "Both of you are Bureau. They'd spot you and suspect anything you did."

"We don't have time to pull in an undercover team," the boss said. "And there's no way to know which of our assets have been turned."

"We could play it straight up," Taylor said slowly.

"Huh?" came from both the tech savvy woman and his boss.

Taylor eyed the technical magician. "Can you get instructions on how to use that ring to the navigator without Alex's gang knowing it?"

"Do bears connect to the net in the woods?" she said with a confident smile. "But you still have to get him the ring."

Now it was Taylor's turn to smile. He keyed his comm-link to a very familiar number. "Love, I need to ask a favor of you. Could you meet me at the space elevator station? I'll be going up, and you may dump on me all of the anger that you have been kind enough to keep to yourself."

"Are you asking for me to argue with you in public?" came back in a dangerously even voice.

"Yes, love."

"That . . . will be a joy," she said, and rang off.

"Is this a good idea?" his boss asked.

"I'll tell you in a week," Taylor said.

They returned to the bureau headquarters. Shortly thereafter, Taylor took public transit to the beanstalk station.

His wife accosted him as he got out at the station.

"Where do you think you're going?" was loaded with all sorts of prickle.

"I have a job up on the station," he said evenly.

"You're on vacation."

"Right after I finish this."

"That's what you told me yesterday, and the day before that and . . ." the argument went on from there, getting louder and more explosive. People took it in . . . and turned away, embarrassed for them. No doubt certain security cameras were also taking it in and conveying it to interested parties.

Taylor did manage to get a few quiet words in. His wife did not pause in her full harridan act, but acknowledged him with a slight widening of her eyes.

Taylor spotted Annie and a very nice looking young man. They easily filled the all too familiar role in the station of lovers about be to parted, and very reluctant to do so.

Taylor slipped the ring into his wife's hands during an attempt to hold her hand and calm her. She slapped him with one hand as she slid the ring onto the small finger of the other.

Taylor waited until the flow of the crowd forced the two couples closer together. He stayed on the far side of his wife from Annie and her boyfriend. His wife chose that moment to turn away from him in full huff.

And ran right into the other couple.

The collision brought on a cascade of falling luggage and a flood of apologies, with several accusatory words and glowers aimed at Taylor for driving her into this personal accident.

Taylor did attempt to say a few words to the couple, but his wife talked over him. When the two younger folks moved on, there was no ring on Taylor's wife's finger.

It was easy to tell, she was wagging one finger of that hand under his nose. "You take your lame ass up that beanstalk and you better bring a lock pick home tonight, 'cause I'll have changed the lock. And I'll have a chain on the door anyway."

"I have to go," Taylor said softly. Firmly. Sadly.

They argued, standing there, impeding traffic, with her holding on tight to his arm and him saying he had to go until the very last warning of the ferry's departure forced him to yank his arm away from her and flee at top speed for the boarding dock, leaving a very angry woman crying in his wake.

I wonder if she had any idea she'd be doing something like that on that long-ago spring day when she said "I do"! Taylor thought as he just barely caught the departing ferry.

Taylor continued playing the senior agent for the trip up. He encountered a full six of the Star Line merchant officers and tried desperately to suborn them. In each case, he failed.

He followed the flow of merchant officers and sailors right up to the gate to the Nuu Yards where a grinning pair was waiting for him.

"You can't go in," Security Agent Cob said, putting a hand on Taylor's chest and shoving him back with a will.

"Yep," Security Specialist Kittikon said. "You ruined my morning. Now I get to ruin your day, month, and year."

"I'll see that the Port Captain withdraws their authorization to sail," Taylor snapped.

"You try," both said with confident grins.

So, Taylor tried. It was amazing how much bureaucracy there was in a space stations port office. He pulled strings. And found that for every string he was pulling on, there were a pair of six inch cables pulling the other way.

Taylor even resorted to trying to have the Navy defense batteries ordered to fire on the ships if they moved. It turned out that the captain with the authority to do that was away from his desk and no one knew when he'd be back.

Clearly, a lot of Alex Longknife's money had gone into getting those ships away from the pier.

At 12:30 pm local they sealed locks. By 1:00 pm they were away, and by 2:00 pm they were out of range of the defense batteries.

It was a well-played charade. For those actually involved in it, Taylor hoped they'd live long enough to spend their bribes. For himself, he hoped the ring and instructions worked as well as advertised.

He was back down the elevator and at his desk when Leslie jumped out of her seat at her desk. "M-688," she whispered. "They're going to M-688."

Taylor called Member of Parliament Honovi Longknife with that information.

"That's a long way away from here," the Longknife scion said. "I've got a squadron of heavy cruisers getting ready to take off after them, but I'm none too sure I can catch them."

"What about calling Kris Longknife?" Leslie put in. "The court is deliberating her fate. If they don't chop off her head, she might be able to do something."

"How?" Mahomet put in. "Even a Longknife needs a spaceship to chase starships."

"Maybe she has one," Leslie shot back. "The school kids on Musashi have been raising money to buy her a ship and go see what the situation is on the planet she tried to save. They're having car washes and bake sales and all sorts of stuff."

"Yeah," Rick said. "That ought to buy her a row boat."

"Actually," her brother said, "it might get her a bit more than that. Mitsubishi is trying something new with Smart Metal. Let me see if Admiral Crossenshield can do something there," the Member of Parliament and the politician who stayed home muttered, half to himself.

Taylor found himself eyeing Leslie. The charter member of the Princess Kris Longknife fan club was grinning from ear to ear.

Taylor set about finishing up loose ends, but his boss came in, took his hat and coat from the stand, and handed them to him. "You go home to your wife. She did a superb job today. I hope it was acting, but I have a bad feeling about it."

Taylor took his offered coat, put his hat on his head and took the trolley home.

The lock had not been changed. His wife met him before he had a chance to close the door with a warm hug and an even warmer kiss.

"That was most cathartic. You must involve me in your work more often," she said slyly. "How'd the rest of your day go?"

"Better than some. Worse than others," he answered in his usual, noncommittal way.

And they might have made a good start on making it a very good day, but the kids chose that moment to storm in from school and the best part of the day had to be put off until later.

Much later, as Taylor held his slumbering wife, he mused on the fortune he had in his family. He found his thoughts roving over what he had discovered of the ups and mostly downs of the Longknife family. He shook his head and wished Kris Longknife better luck with family in the future than she seemed to have had so far in her young life.

ABOUT THE AUTHOR

Mike Shepherd is the National best-selling author of the Kris Longknife saga. Mike Moscoe is the award nominated short story writer who has also written several novels, most of which were, until recently, out of print. Though the two have never been seen in the same room at the same time, they are reported to be good friends.

Mike Shepherd grew up Navy. It taught him early about change and the chain of command. He's worked as a bartender and cab driver, personnel advisor and labor negotiator. Now retired from building databases about the endangered critters of the Northwest, he's looking forward to some fun reading and writing.

Mike lives in Vancouver, Washington, with his wife Ellen, and not too far from his daughter and grandkids. He enjoys reading, writing, dreaming, watching grand-children for story ideas and upgrading his computer – all are never ending.

For more information:
www.mikeshepherd.org
mikeshepherd@krislongknife.com

2017 RELEASES

In 2016, I amicably ended my twenty-year publishing relationship with Ace, part of Penguin Random House.

In 2017, I began publishing through my own independent press, KL & MM Books.

I am delighted to say that you fans have responded wonderfully. We have sold over 20,000 copies of the five e-novels. In 2018, I intend to keep the novels coming,

We started the year with **Kris Longknife's Replacement** that tells the story of Grand Admiral Sandy Santiago as she does her best as a mere mortal to fill the shoes left behind on Alwa Station by Kris Longknife. Sandy has problems galore: birds, cats, and vicious alien raiders. Oh, and she's got Rita Nuu-Longknife as well!

February had a novelette. **Kris Longknife: Among the Kicking Birds** was part of Kris Longknife: Unrelenting. However, it went long and these four chapters were cut to one short paragraph. I hope you enjoy the full story.

Rita Longknife: Enemy Unknown was available in March and is the first book of the long-awaited Iteeche War series. Rita has had enough of Ray Longknife gallivanting around the universe. No sooner is little Al born, than ships start disappearing. Is it pirates or something more sinister? Rita gets herself command of a heavy cruiser, some nannies, and heads out to see what there is to see.

April had another short offering, **Kris Longknife's Bad Day**. You just knew when Kris asked for a desk job that she'd have days like you have at the office. Well, here's one that will bring you up to date on the technical developments in the Royal US Navy, as well as silly bureaucratic goings on. In the first draft of **Emissary**, these were the opening chapters, but I found a better opening and this got cut. Enjoy!

Kris Longknife: Emissary began an entirely new story arc for Kris and was available May 1. Here is the story of what it takes to get Kris out from behind a desk. And for those of you betting in the pool, you'll get your answer. More I cannot say.

June brought you Abby Nightingale's view of things around Alwa in **Kris Longknife's Maid Goes on Strike.** You knew sooner or later this was going to happen.

July had another book set in Alwa. As **Kris Longknife's Relief,** Sandy Santiago, continues to battle aliens of various persuasions and not a few humans.

Rita Longknife: Enemy in Sight was released in September and sought to resolve the unknowns left by Enemy Unknown as humanity slipped backwards into a war it does not want and may not be able to win.

Kris Longknife's Maid Goes on Strike and Other Short Stories, is a collection of four short stories: Maid Goes on Strike, Ruthie Longknife's First Christmas, Among the Kicking Birds, and Bad Day. These were available in October all under one ebook cover for a great price.

Kris Longknife: Admiral was available in November. In this adventure, Kris is up to her ears in warships, enemies, and friendlies who may be not as friendly as she'd like, as battlecruisers square off against battlecruisers. A fight where both sides are equal is a bloody fight that often no one wins.

Work is already going on for a February 1 release of Kris Longknife's Successor. March will have the next book in the Iteeche War, and May will continue Kris's adventures in the Iteeche Empire with Kris Longknife: Warrior.

Stay in touch to follow developments by following Kris Longknife on Facebook or checking in at my website www.mikeshepherd.org.

I hope to soon have a mailing list you can sign up for.

Printed in Great Britain
by Amazon